T0334751

BISON
BOOKS

THE PINTO HORSE

and

THE PHANTOM BULL

Charles Elliott Perkins

ILLUSTRATIONS BY EDWARD BOREIN

Introduction to the Bison Books Edition
by Jay Fultz

UNIVERSITY OF NEBRASKA PRESS
LINCOLN AND LONDON

∞

First Bison Books printing: 1998

Library of Congress Cataloging-in-Publication Data
Perkins, Charles Elliott, 1881–1943.
[Pinto horse]
The pinto horse; and, The phantom bull / Charles Elliott Perkins; illustrations by Edward Borein; introduction to the Bison Books edition by Jay Fultz.
p. cm.
"The Pinto horse" was originally published in 1927. "The Phantom bull," originally published in 1932.
Includes bibliographical references.
ISBN 0-8032-8752-6 (pbk.: alk. paper)
1. Horses. 2. Cattle. I. Perkins, Charles Elliott, 1881–1943. Phantom bull. II. Title. III. Title: Phantom bull.
QL795.H7P4 1998
636.1—dc21
98-36712 CIP

The Pinto Horse reprinted from the original 1927 edition by Wallace Hebberd, Santa Barbara CA. *The Phantom Bull* reprinted from the original 1932 edition by Houghton Mifflin Company, Boston.

INTRODUCTION

Jay Fultz

The name Charles Elliot Perkins used to resound in the tomes devoted to America's authentic big shots. The *National Cyclopedia of American Biography* included a full-page photograph of him, looking handsome in his square-faced Warren Harding way and more like a funeral director than a railroadman and rancher.[1]

Perkins was born (in Burlington, Iowa, 1881) with a golden spike in his mouth, so to speak. His father, also C. E., was president of the Chicago, Burlington & Quincy Railroad during the Gilded Age. Later on, the son would run the same railway, and several others as well.

Although rooted in Massachusetts and Harvard-bred, young Perkins, like his father, grew an empire in the Middle and Mountain West. When the old man died in 1907, Charley, as he was known in Iowa, took over and further developed far-flung land and cattle companies. (In 1909 the Perkins family deeded the scenic Garden of the Gods to the state of Colorado.) During World War I, Charley presided over the CB&Q, the Colorado & Southern, the Fort Worth & Denver City, and the Wichita Valley lines. After the war, he was president of two banks in Burlington.

If Charley's head was in business, his heart was in raising thoroughbred horses and purebred cattle. In the 1920s the Perkins farm south of Burlington was famous for its high-class hunting and jumping horses, which were shipped to Virginia and to England for chasing the fox. Sharing the pasture were Hereford steers imported from the Matador range in Texas. Then, in 1927, Charley moved to Santa Barbara, California, and bought the ten-thousand-acre Alisal Ranch in the Santa Ynez Valley. Among its distinguished residents was Flying Ebony, the 1925 winner of the Kentucky Derby.

That year, 1927, revealed the storyteller in the business executive and stockman. Every night Charley told western yarns to his children, who were so captivated that Mrs. Perkins suggested he collect and publish them. He wove them into a narrative titled *The Pinto Horse* and approached a friend in Santa

Barbara, the publisher Wallace Hebberd. What Perkins intended as a book just for the family became an ambitious literary project when Hebberd recognized the quality of the writing. Hebberd, who edited the manuscript, wanted the prestigious R. R. Donnelley & Sons Company in Chicago as printer. The celebrated author of *The Virginian*, Owen Wister, was enlisted to write a foreword. And Edward Borein, who lived in Santa Barbara and had drawn for magazines and newspapers but never before for a book, was set to illustrate.

The result was "a rarely beautiful book," as J. Frank Dobie described it in *Southwest Review*.[2] *The Pinto Horse* is animal biography of distinctive clarity and grace. Perkins resists the easy habit of humanizing his four-footed subject. The spotted horse that survives on the Montana range in the 1880s is always a horse, a perfect blend of mustang and thoroughbred. The sentimentality of Anna Sewell's *Black Beauty* is missing in *The Pinto Horse*, as well as the sometimes tiresome cowboy vernacular of Will James's *Smoky*. In fact, men and women, who readily enter the kingdom of *My Friend Flicka* by Mary O'Hara, don't dominate *The Pinto Horse*. In the end, Pinto completely loses touch with humans, for good reason.

The pinto has been in North America since the sixteenth century, when Spanish explorers brought a band of horses to the continent. The breed has sacrificed its fair share to American history. "At the Alamo, the Fetterman massacre, the Battle of the Little Big Horn, the paint horse was there," writes Glynn W. Haynes.[3]

Many people think of the particolored pinto as a smallish horse, similar to the Indian pony. But through crossbreeding, pintos gained size and strength. Pinto in Perkins's story has "the superb physique of his thoroughbred English mother, combined with the wiry toughness of his wild father." His black and white splendor makes him a target for thieves of every stripe.

The western Indian tribes especially valued the pinto or paint for its showiness. Going into battle, they decorated their horses, and the pinto was naturally colorful. Paradoxically, the Indians also sought the pinto for purposes of camouflage: it was easy to alter or paint over the spots so that both rider and horse merged into the background colors of the changing seasons.[4]

Cattlemen valued the pinto much less. It was generally not considered a good cow horse, being unsuited for close, quick work.[5] (However, the pinto in Ralph Moody's *Home Ranch* is a decent cutting horse. Perhaps significantly, it is ridden by a brash girl who is the nemesis of the young Ralph.)

In packing off Pinto to the Billings Fair (and later to England, where he runs to the hounds in Belvoir Vale), Perkins suggests the fate of such horses when the day of the open range passed. They survived conspicuously as performers in the Wild West shows that began in the 1880s and lasted until the 1920s. Then came the rodeos, where their special toughness was required. Then the movies: the first cowboy star, William S. Hart, rode a pinto named Fritz.

Though part of Americana and drawn by artists like Charles Russell, the pinto had to wait for Charles Elliott Perkins to register strongly in literature. It does seem that the most famous horses in children's books are anything but pintos. Black Beauty, Smoky, Thunderhead, Flicka, Old Slate, the racer in Enid Bagnold's *National Velvet*—all tend to be uniform in color.

Still favored by authors is the fiery wild stallion, often white like O'Hara's Thunderhead, or brown like Rival in Jo Sykes's *Saddle a Thunderbolt*, or ebony like the Black Stallion in the series of books by Walter Farley. Certainly a wingless Pegasus or Bucephalus will electrify more readers than a farm nag. But the truly beautiful wild stallion remembered from storybooks is largely a fiction, according to Walker D. Wyman. "When found at all [it] proved to be a blooded stray that had escaped from some rancher's domestic stock," he writes in *The Wild Horse of the West*.[6] Thus, Perkins's pinto stallion, blooded by half, may have more legitimate claim to magnificence than some wildings of literary renown.

Like many animal stories, *The Pinto Horse* ends in the realm of legend. "The Painted Moonbeam" belongs to Indian lore, and possibly Perkins was also thinking of the Ghost Horse of the Plains, a fabled white steed that was reported by travelers from Texas to Montana for sixty years.[7] Deepened by this extra dimension, *The Pinto Horse* is nonetheless (as J. Frank Dobie noted) "so realistic and natural that the book is good for sheer narrative."[8] And Owen Wister, in the foreword included here, found "nothing made-up, faked" in it. A man who knew horses has forever caught them as they lived in southern Montana in the later 1880s, when the range was still open to the Canadian line, when longhorn cattle were pouring in from Texas and Englishmen were vested ranchers, when the vigilantes were terrorizing thieves and the bones of livestock were signs of a recent killer winter.

The artistic, if not commercial, success of *The Pinto Horse* assured that a major house, Houghton Mifflin, would publish *The Phantom Bull* in 1932. The volumes are companions, linked by the Montana setting, time (both begin in 1888), the author's knowledge of animal nature, his felicity of language, and Edward Borein's illustrations.

The country of *The Pinto Horse* is north of Billings, in present-day Yellowstone and Musselshell counties, while that of *The Phantom Bull* is to the west, in the valleys of the Madison and Gallatin rivers. The domains are close, dramatically as well as geographically, and the pinto is brought over to chase the runaway bull.

For most readers, bulls don't have quite the emotional appeal of horses and dogs. (An exception is the peaceful Ferdinand, the bull in Munro Leaf's delightful fable that is mistaken as fierce when he reacts to a bee sting.) But the splash-faced bull in Perkins's story, wild beyond words, is more sympathetic than the ranchers who try to capture him. (Chief among them is "Old Man Ennis," important to Montana history as William Ennis, a pioneer stockman in the Madison Valley and founder of the town of Ennis.)

When the scene shifts to a Mexican bullring, the reader roots for the surly Phantom Bull instead of the Spanish matador, so skillfully has Perkins established the animal's point of view without anthropomorphizing it. Here the meaning of the ritual celebrated by Ernest Hemingway has been inverted, for in *his* world the bull has no point of view, not even tangentially; no value except to bring out the matador's "grace" and "courage" before he kills it. The obligatory death of the bull is, for humans, a momentary triumph over death. Incidentally, the matador in *The Phantom Bull* is called El Gallo. That name was used professionally by the great Gomez family of Gypsy bullfighters.[9] Perkins sees nothing to admire in his El Gallo, who may be purely fictional. By contrast, the latter-day real El Gallo of Hemingway's *Death in the Afternoon* is a paragon of skill and dignity.

As a livestock breeder Perkins knew the odds of survival. The arena of *The Pinto Horse* and *The Phantom Bull* is elemental; the strongest and sleekest seem to invite violence. Perkins comes close in sensibility to the robust but highly literate Theodore Roosevelt, and it is easy to imagine the businessman-cum-rancher on a sanguinary safari with his dead-shot contemporary. Yet his love of animals is abundantly evident in the only two books he ever wrote.

The dynamic illustrations by Edward Borein help lift the books to the level of art. After years of cowboying and drawing for popular magazines and advertisements, Borein built a studio in Santa Barbara, California. This was in 1921, six years before Perkins moved there. The artist and the author, both visual storytellers who valued realistic detail, were surely destined to meet. Perkins died in 1943; Borein, two years later.

Today Edward Borein is ranked with Frederic Remington and Charles Russell as a western artist. Justly so. Charles Elliott Perkins has been forgotten—unjustly because *The Pinto Horse* and *The Phantom Bull* are works of historical and artistic integrity. They are small classics, long lost to readers until now.

NOTES

1. "Perkins, Charles Elliott," in *National Cyclopedia of American Biography* (New York: James T. White & Co., 1945), 32: 24–26.

2. J. Frank Dobie, review of *The Pinto Horse* by Charles Elliott Perkins, *Southwest Review*, 14, no. 3 (spring 1929): xvi.

3. Glynn W. Haynes, *The American Paint Horse* (Norman: University of Oklahoma Press, 1976), 27.

4. Haynes, *American Paint Horse*, 24–25.

5. John M. Hendrix, "Paints as Cow Horses," *The Cattleman*, November 1934, 13.

6. Walker D. Wyman, *The Wild Horse of the West* (Caldwell ID: Caxton Printers, Ltd., 1945), 306.

7. Hope Ryden, *America's Last Wild Horses* (New York: E. P. Dutton & Co., 1970), 131; J. Frank Dobie, *The Mustangs* (Boston: Little, Brown & Co., 1952), 155.

8. Dobie, review of *The Pinto Horse*, xvi.

9. Ernest Hemingway, *Death in the Afternoon* (London: Jonathan Cape, 1932), 290.

The Pinto Horse

Foreword

By Owen Wister

This is the best Western story about a horse, that I have ever read; which need not mean either that the reader will agree with me, or that no better story exists. A very distinguished publisher did not agree with me; he feared that it would not interest many readers.

From start to finish it interested me for these reasons:

It was so true to the cow-puncher West, that no one who had not himself lived that life thoroughly and intimately could possibly have written it; throughout there is nothing made-up, faked; nothing transplanted into the soil of the sage-brush that in fact grows somewhere else. And there is no false sentiment. The horse remains a horse, never becomes half-human with thoughts and emotions no horse could have.

I do not know the author, have never even seen him. He does not write as a born author, perhaps may never try it again. But he has the power of natural, direct expression, and has used this to tell of a life which he must have lived with all the enthusiasm of youth.

Owen Wister

The Pinto Horse

CHAPTER I

In the Spring of '88, "Patch" was running a band of Oregon mares in the Bull Mountains of Southern Montana. The Bull Mountains are a range of high and broken hills, sparsely covered with jack pine, and heavily grassed in the open parks, with springs at the coulee heads; an ideal winter range for horses. On the south, the country falls away in lessening grassy ridges twenty miles to the Yellowstone. To the north, it drops more steeply to the Mussel Shell Flats.

In those days, the country north of the Yellowstone had not been restocked after the terrible winter of '86, the range was all open to the Canadian Line, and the native grass grew in its natural abundance.

From May to November the mares were divided into two bands; one which ranged south to the Yellowstone; the other, to the north of the Bull Mountain hills. Each Spring, the Honorable William Spencer Fitzhenry Wantage, third son of the Earl of Palmadime, brought up from his ranch on Powder River the thoroughbred stallions that were to run with the mares; each November he came for them. In the meantime, all Patch had to do was to ride each morning from his cabin in the foot-hills, locate his mares, count them, and once a week cross over to the other side of the hills to see that his assistant, Mr. "Slippery Bill" Weston, and the mares that he looked after were in good order. It was a pleasant life; twice a week the Billings stage left the mail in a tin box on the Yellowstone Trail, and once a month Patch hooked up his mule team and drove into Billings for supplies. That trip took three days, and always Patch came back strapped, but happy.

In the Autumn, when the stallions had gone back to Powder River, the horses of both bands were brought together to the corrals at the head of Big Coulee, the weanlings branded, the geldings that were to be broken, cut out and turned into the saddle-horse pasture, and the balance of the herd turned loose again to winter in the hills.

Range horses know the seasons as well as man, and they know their range as no man ever knows it. They know the pockets where the Northers never strike; they know where the warm springs are that never freeze, and they know which ridges are exposed to the Chinooks—warm winds that melt the snow. The range horse loves its native range as no other animal loves its home, and will return to it hundreds of miles, if it has the chance. Especially is this true of mares, which never forget the range where their first foal is dropped. Once a mare has foaled, she will spend the rest of her life within a radius of a few miles, if there is enough feed and water.

The first autumn and winter that Patch had the Oregon mares, he spent all the days and many freezing nights riding to turn them back in their drift toward the West.

When Patch and the Hon. Wm. Spencer Fitzhenry Wantage, who owned a half interest in the horses, were bringing the mares from Oregon, their regular pack horse went lame and they caught what seemed a quiet mare to pack in its place. They haltered the mare and tied her to a tree, packed on her their bedding and cook outfit, and then, as she seemed frightened by the pack sheet, the Honorable, thinking to get her used to it, tied one end to the front of the pack saddle, and with a corner of the other end in each hand, stood behind her and gave it a flap. The result was electric.

The mare broke away and dashed down the road, the loose sheet flying and flapping above her like a cloud. The first thing she struck was the band of mares, which scattered far and wide; the next thing she ran into was a herd of beef being driven to the railroad; these stampeded like the mares. There were two drummers driving out from town, with a pair, in a top buggy. The flying mare met them head on. The team jack-knifed, broke the pole and a drummer's leg, and disappeared like the beef steers and the mares, while she pursued her unhallowed course into town, wrecked a mounted pageant of the Knights of Columbus, threw the Grand Knight through the plate glass window of the Masonic Hall, and finally fell down herself in the public square.

Patch and the Honorable Wm. Spencer Fitzhenry Wantage spent the next two days rounding up all of the scattered mares that they could find. Twelve they never got, and of these, nine eventually found their way back from Montana to the range in Oregon where they were foaled, *eight hundred miles away*, swimming the Snake River to get there.

So Patch was looking after the band of mares on the Bull Mountain range, when one morning in June, he rode out to locate them, and to see if Stowaway, the thoroughbred stallion which had begun his first season on the range a month before, was all right. Over the grassy ridges he jogged, whistling "Garryowen," while the larks, out of sight above, poured down a stream of song. He had found the band the day before and knew, if nothing had disturbed them, he would find them again a few miles further on toward the Yellowstone. Sure enough, when he was still two miles away, he saw them feeding on a little flat along the Cottonwood. But before he reached them, crossing a dry wash, he came upon Stowaway, covered with blood and carrying all the marks of battle, too lame and sore to climb out of the shallow gully into which he had staggered.

TWICE A WEEK THE BILLINGS STAGE LEFT THE MAIL IN A TIN BOX ON

Patch knew it meant that some range stallion had found the band, nearly killed Stowaway, and taken them for himself. That must be seen to. He kicked his pony into a gallop, but before he had come within one hundred yards of the grazing mares, a black and white spotted stallion came snorting out to meet him. Indian, thought Patch, escaped from some band of Crows off their reservation south of the Yellowstone, or else a wanderer driven from some herd of Crow horses which had smelled the mares from miles across the river and come over to get a harem of his own. On came the pinto stallion, ears back, mouth open, until within twenty yards, Patch untied his slicker and swung it around his head. The wild horse slid to a stop, stamped, snorted and trotted back to the mares.

It was lucky for him that the cowboy feared Indians might be camped nearby, or a bullet from his forty-five would have ended the career of that spotted Don Juan there and then, for thoroughbred stallions were scarcer on the Montana Range than feathered frogs, and Patch was mad; it would take Stowaway weeks to get over his beating. What was to be done? He could not shoot the pinto. For, though the Indians were peaceful enough at home, they did not leave their reservation unless they were up to some mischief; and in killing a lone cowboy, and stealing his horse and guns there would be no great risk of discovery, in that unsettled country. There was nothing for it but to start the mares quietly up the creek toward the corrals, twelve miles away at the winter camp at the head of Big Coulee; the wild stallion would go with them, and once started Patch knew that they would head straight for the corrals where they were regularly salted. So, with one eye over his shoulder in case of an Indian surprise, he worked his way to the lower side of the herd, careful to keep below the rim of the encircling hills.

The Indian stallion dashed to and fro, snorting, always between

Patch and the mares, but the flying slicker kept him from attacking the saddle horse, and gradually the cowboy got near enough to turn one grazing mare and then another, until he had the whole band slowly walking up the creek. For a mile they strolled on, feeding as they went, and then, as they got far enough away so that the dust would not be noticed, Patch crowded the last ones until they began to jog and then to gallop. After another mile he knew he had them fully roused, and that they would not stop or turn until they got to the corrals.

Then Patch pulled up and watched them out of sight—the wild stallion turning to snort and stamp once more before he disappeared after the mares. The cowboy loped back down the creek, and cutting across to where Stowaway was still standing in the dry wash, dropped his rope over the stallion's head and started with him to the home camp; but the battered horse went slowly, and it was mid-afternoon when Patch left him in the shade of some alders half a mile from the corrals. There, as he hoped, he found the mares, some licking salt, some rolling in the dust, the pinto stallion just inside the gate. Patch knew that the only way to get rid of him was to scare him so badly that he would go back to his own range, and to do that he would have to catch him. He could not keep the mares in the corral; there was no feed, and if the stallion were not badly scared he would stay in the broken country nearby, and wait until the mares came out. Patch slipped off his horse and crept nearer; the stallion did not wind him, and he got within ten yards, screened by some chokeberry bushes.

Then with a yell he started. The wild horse saw him the fraction of a second too late, and the heavy gate slammed in his face as he reared against it. The rest was simple; the pinto was roped, thrown, and hog-tied, and a lard pail full of stones, the top wired on, tied to his tail. The mares were penned in the second corral, the gate thrown open, the tie-ropes loosed, and the terrified stallion crashed off down the draw, the lard pail banging at his hocks.

That night, thirty miles to the south, the sleeping Indians on the Little Horn clutched each other in terror, and their frightened ponies scattered to the hills.

THE TEAM JACK-KNIFED (PAGE 3)

CHAPTER II

One May morning, when Patch was counting the mares, a year after he had tied the lard pail to the painted stallion, he missed Bald Stockings, a thoroughbred English mare that the Honorable Wantage had turned on the range with Stowaway. Patch did not try to find her, but a week later as he went to get his saddle horse in the morning, he found her in the corral licking salt, and beside her a wobbly-legged pinto foal. Bald Stockings snorted and trotted to the far end of the corral as Patch shut the gate. For half an hour he could not get near her, but he knew horses; so for the first few minutes he sat on the fence and whistled, and gradually as the mare quieted, he strolled nearer, until he could rub her nose, and then her neck; then he left her and went about his day's work.

Late that afternoon he tried again, and this time with little trouble he haltered her, and soon the foal, too, would allow him to scratch its back. For a week Patch kept the mare in the hay corral, and by that time the foal would follow him about and lick his hand for sugar. The pinto colt started life with confidence in man, and Hinton knew that some day that confidence would save him much trouble. Later, the mare joined the band, and each day when Patch counted them, he gave the foal some sugar. Before the end of the summer it would leave the band and trot to meet him when he whistled the first few bars of "The Spanish Cavalier."

Bald Stockings was a good mother; the colt grew fast, and as the summer drifted by he learned the lessons of the range: how to stick close to his mother's side, so as not to be stepped on or knocked down when the band of mares was galloping; how to give Stowaway a wide berth; how to keep one eye always on the watch for prairie dog holes; and also about wolves—that was a terrifying experience. One hot noon, Pinto lay stretched out asleep on a hill-side; Bald Stockings gradually had grazed on fifty yards down the swale. The foal never knew exactly what happened. There was a snarling rush which knocked him over as he scrambled to his feet. He heard his mother squeal, and the next thing he knew she was striking and biting at a gray thing that writhed on the grass, while another gray streak vanished over the ridge. It was over in a minute, and the mare, with nostrils flaring and a red light in her great wild eye, was nuzzling the still dazed foal. The gray thing on the grass was still; but before they trotted off to join the band the big mare shook it like a rag, while the foal huddled against her. And ever afterwards, when he smelt the wolf smell, he remembered; and when he was older, he would follow it to kill, sometimes with success, until no wolf of that range would come near any band of horses that the pinto ran with.

September came and went; the long strings of wild geese went honking over-head, and the quaking aspen had yellowed in the gulches, when one morning two men, strange to Pinto, helped Patch drive the band of horses to the big corrals. There Pinto was whistled from the band, and there was much talk that he did not understand. Then he and Bald Stockings were driven into a smaller corral where they waited, snorting, while the dust went up in clouds in the main corral, and the smell of burning flesh and hair added terror to the shouts of men, the wild calls of the mares, and the squeals of branded foals. Pinto did not know until long after that Patch had bought the Hon. Wantage's half interest in him, and had declared he should never be disfigured with a brand.

Late that afternoon, with the first winter storm breaking over-head, when the band of mares was turned out and driven into the foot-hills to their winter range, Bald Stockings and Pinto were turned into the saddle-horse pasture with the geldings, and there Pinto spent his first winter, feeding on the buffalo grass, when the Chinooks swept the ridges clear, warm and snug in the hay corral when a wild Norther roared down from the Canadas. And always he kept learning; for every few days Patch whistled him from the others to give him a bite of sugar or a piece of bread, so that he never had the range-horse's fear of man.

From the wise old geldings, he learned to find the least windy spots along the wind-swept hill-sides; he learned how to paw through the crust and get the sweet grass underneath, when the strongest bull would have starved, for no member of the cow family has learned to break the crust with its feet, and so, when it cannot push through the snow with its nose, it dies, where a range horse fattens. He learned something, too, of the tactics of war; for the veteran geldings would fight like wolves for a warm pocket in which to feed, or a specially sheltered nook near the hay stacks, on the bitter winter nights when the sky over the Mussel Shell shivered with the Northern Lights. Once there was an attack of wolves, but the geldings, without excitement, almost with indifference, headed in a circle, in the center of which were Bald Stockings and Pinto, presenting an unbroken battery of heels, which only one rash wolf dared venture, only to be hurled back, a broken thing, and torn to pieces by his ravening friends. Bald Stockings was for breaking out into open attack, but the sour old geldings knew better and met her with flattened ears and clicking teeth, and the wolves, half fed on their foolish companion, slunk away.

SHE WAS STRIKING AND BITING AT A GRAY THING (PAGE 10)

CHAPTER III

And so the winter passed, until one morning, while snow still lay in the deeper gulches, Bald Stocking and Pinto again found themselves in the small corral from which they had neighed good-bye to the brood mare band the autumn before. Again came the two strangers, leading Stowaway; again, the big corral was filled with dust and squeals, but this time there was no smell of burning, and the squeals held a different note. That afternoon when the band was turned out, Bald Stockings and Pinto went with them, while Stowaway, like a king, trotted here and there, nipping a careless yearling that crossed his path, courted by some mares, but met by Bald Stockings with a swish of her thin tail and a warning snap of her white teeth.

In a few days, the life of the last summer was resumed, but not until Pinto had, in the meantime, established his standing with the colts and fillies of his own age. He was the only pinto among them, and half a hand taller than the biggest—the good blue-stem hay eaten through the winter, plus an inheritance from his tall English mother, accounted for that. For the first day, the other yearlings, all intimate friends from their long winter together, amused themselves by chasing Pinto in wide circles around the band of feeding mares, and, for a time, this seemed to Pinto good sport, for he found he could easily out-gallop them, but at last, getting out of wind—they had chased him in relays—he stopped and faced them.

A woolly brown colt, the leader, with a head like Stowaway's, walked out to fight him. Pinto stretched out his neck for a friendly touching of noses, and received, to his surprise, a cruel slash across the throat. He screamed, and instinctively looked around for his mother's help. Bald Stockings, feeding only a few yards off, looked up and then went on grazing. Then something moved inside of Pinto that he had never felt before; his ears went back along his head, and he went for that woolly yearling like a painted wild-cat. It was not in vain he had watched the vicious old geldings fight for a warm spot on the windy side-hills, or for those snug corners near the hay-stacks in the bitter winter nights. Squealing, biting, striking, he hurled himself at the other colt. The latter, trying to turn and run for it, was knocked flat, screaming, while the painted devil, his fore-feet beating like flails, tore at the brown throat. It was going too far. The brown colt's mother raced up with squealing fury, only to be met by Bald Stockings, a demon now herself. Another battle was started, when Stowaway rushed the mares apart and drove Pinto cowering to his mother, a bleeding wound in his rump.

A range stallion is absolute king of his band, until some other stallion beats him in open fight; and from then on he is never allowed to approach it. That fight, however, established Pinto as the yearlings' leader. He would lead them to the top of some grassy ridge, and then pretending to be frightened, he would turn and come racing back ahead of them to the herd. He had tremendous fake fights with the other colts, rearing, striking, biting and whirling to kick, all in rough play, while the fillies stood about admiring. And then one night, while he was asleep, Bald Stockings vanished. For a day and a night, the homesick colt walked the ridges, calling; going as far as he dared, alone, from the band. But no answer came, and when Patch rode up the second morning, Pinto followed him on his day's round. That night the cowboy fed the tired yearling in the corral, and next day, turned him with his old friends, the saddle-horses. Most men would have tried to drive him back to the herd, but Hinton was that rarest of men, a cowboy, and a really fine horseman, who understood horses in all their phases. He knew what would happen, and not for anything would he have risked losing the pinto's confidence.

Sure enough, a few mornings later, Bald Stockings was again licking salt in the big corral; but this time with a brown foal instead of a pinto, by her side. When Pinto was let in from the saddle-horse pasture, he ran to her whinneying with delight, but the big mare kept between him and the foal, and when Pinto, in his curiosity to investigate the strange wobbly brown thing, tried to push past her, he was met with a gleam of teeth that he understood meant "no crowding," and gradually, as they joined the herd, his jealous disappointment vanished, and he was soon leading the other yearlings, as before; but now he was more independent of his mother, although he always lay down near her, and when the band was moving, always kept where he could see her.

By mid-summer, Pinto was as big as the average well-bred two-year-old, and, except for his coloring, bore no trace of the painted Indian stallion that two years before had wrecked the peace of a June night and frightened the Plains animals from the Big Coulee to the Little Horn. The lean, game head; the great, brown eyes, with a touch of wildness; the thin, tapering, mobile ears; the deep chest; the shoulders raking far back; the powerful, arched loins; the thin, high-set tail, and broad quarters, heavily muscled to the hocks, were all an inheritance of his English ancestors. While the brain, that was developing behind that thin-skinned bony forehead, was that of a courageous and intelligent thoroughbred horse, combined with the alert and instinctive cunning of a wild animal, ever ready to meet the emergency which always comes to the wild things. Patch Hinton realized that so perfect an animal, driven by such a brain, would, if wisely handled, develop into a horse matchless in the cow country, from California to the Missouri, from Alberta to the Gulf.

PINTO WAS WHISTLED FROM THE BAND (PAGE 10)

CHAPTER IV

L, Patch was not the only one on the range that recognized the pinto as a gem, even among that fine band of half-bred colts. But both the colt and Patch would have been saved much grief if his color had been bay, or black, or chestnut, for a "paint" colt, with Pinto's size and quality, stood out from the others as the Indian paint-brush in the mountain meadows stands out from the grass around it.

One morning, as the horses were grazing near the mouth of the Cottonwood, where the stage road crosses a grassy bench, there passed up the road on the way from the reservation to the Billings Fair, five Crow bucks, mounted on their best ponies and decked out in the height of Indian gala dress. A hundred yards behind the bucks, jingled a battered hearse, driven by Two Leggings' oldest and most wrinkled wife; while lying down inside, two younger wives gazed through its glass sides on the passing scene. A proud man was Two Leggings, who had bought the hearse the year before from Ed Taintor, the Billings livery man, and proud were his three wives who thus were going to the Fair in style, while other squaws were left on the reservation.

Now a Plains Indian counts his wealth in horses, and a pinto horse is to him what a blue diamond must have been to the elder Mr. Tiffany. The bucks turned off the road to look at the horses, and the hearse jerked to a stop. Stowaway stepped out with a challenging snort between the Indians and the mares, and stopped to look at the bright colored cavalcade. Pinto, less fearful than the rest, trotted past him to investigate, until, catching the Indian scent on an eddy of the morning breeze, he whirled with a snort of terror, which communicating itself to the band, set them galloping up the Cottonwood bottoms in a cloud of dust. But the damage had been done. The Indians sat their ponies in silence, until the horses were out of sight, and then there broke out a guttural torrent of Crow admiration for the pinto colt. He was an antelope for swiftness, a buffalo for strength, a mountain lion for grace. Surely no one-eyed white man could be allowed to keep such a horse. He was unbranded, and, therefore, a maverick, and the property of the first man who marked him for his own. Clearly, the Fair must be given up. The Indians knew that Hinton would go to it. They had seen him there before. They would go quietly to a spring tucked away two or three miles up the valley of the Cottonwood, and wait there until a scouting buck watched Patch well on his way. Orders were shouted to the hearse. The line of march headed up the creek, while the old squaw from the box seat thoroughly, but silently, cursed all pinto horses, and the inside passengers pounded on the glass.

That was on Sunday, and Patch rode over to see what Mr. Weston might wish for in Billings. Monday morning before daylight, he had saddled up. By eight, he was back at his cabin, having located and counted the horses. By ten, shaved and dressed in his store clothes, he was mounting the seat of his spring wagon. By noon the watching Crow, Iron Horse, twelve miles on the Billings road, was untying his hidden pony to hurry back to the camp on Cottonwood and report the coast clear.

Meanwhile, Patch jogged on towards Billings, full of pleasant anticipations; the meeting with old friends, the making of new, the horse races, the Ball over the general store, the lights, the brass foot-rail, the clink of glasses and the click of chips. He was too old now to enter the riding contest. But, perhaps, if he felt first-rate—and his mind went back with a thrill to the day in Abilene when he was twenty; the day before he lost his eye; the day when he won the silver mounted saddle; and he wondered whatever had become of the Swedish biscuit-shooter with the pulled-candy hair in the Gem Restaurant. He hit the off-mule hard, and the sunburn on his wrinkled neck grew a shade redder as he thought of the way she had quit him for that damned Chicago drummer, when he lost his eye. The off-mule grunted—he had not been in Abilene—and Iron Horse quirted his pony across the hills, for no time must be lost in putting as many miles as possible between then and the time when Hinton would came jogging back to count his mares.

Meanwhile, camp was broken on the Cottonwood, the younger squaws and the scanty supplies packed, and the hearse with the old squaw on the box was bumping its way towards the ford on the Yellowstone, with instructions to camp on a certain creek on the reservation. By the time Iron Horse got back to report, only Two Leggings remained, the three others having been sent to locate and watch the band of horses. In those days the Indians had not learned to use saddles, and consequently could not rope from a horse as the cowboys did; it would have been an impossible job for them to capture the pinto yearling, who could out-gallop and out-last the Indian ponies; and to drive him off with a number of other horses would make the whole thing too conspicuous to keep hidden. The colt must be caught, and taken out of the country quickly and alone, and Two Leggings had a bright idea. It would be a simple matter to drive the horses to the home corrals, where they went whenever disturbed, and once in the corrals, the rest would be easy. Of course, Mr. Slippery Weston might show up and give things an unpleasant turn, but it was not likely that anything would bring him across from his part of the range before Wednesday, when he would come over to locate and count the horses, pending Hinton's return.

Iron Horse and Two Leggings joined the watchers, and then

FIVE CROW BUCKS, MOUNTED ON THEIR BEST PONIES (PAGE 17)

with a yell and much waving of blankets, burst over a little hill, below which the horses were feeding. Away went the band straight to the corrals, not even Stowaway stopping for his usual defiant parade. They were there ten minutes ahead of the galloping Indians, and when Two Leggings shut the gate, they were trapped, and at the Indians' mercy—trapped by the very means that Hinton thought insured their safety. For in that open, unfenced country, they would have been comparatively safe from capture.

The Indians climbed the fence and feasted their horse-hungry eyes on the finest band of horses they had ever seen, and especially on the black and white colt, which, with the instinct of a wild animal, tried to hide himself by pushing into the thickest of the mob. Then Two Leggings manned the gate between the corrals, and as the frantic horses milled about in the dust, he opened it a little, until, by twos and threes, they dashed through the half open gate, only too glad to escape from the sight and smell of the shouting Indians in front. Each time Pinto tried to pass, the big gate slammed in his face, until only one other colt was left with him. Two Leggings hooked the gate and took his stand, rope in hand, in the middle of the main corral, while the two maddened youngsters raced around him. He threw and missed. He threw again, and the flying rope missed the pinto's head by an inch, and was kicked off his flying quarters high in the air He threw a third time, and, as the noose fell true, took a quick turn around the snubbing post set in the center of the corral. The rawhide tightened with a twang and stretched a little as the flying pinto reared against it and then came over backward with a crash. Dazed for a second by the fall, the colt lay still and Standing Bear roped both hind legs, and with the help of the others, stretched him flat and helpless. To slip on a rope halter, to make another rope fast to his tail, took only a minute, and then the heel ropes were loosed, the choking rope around his neck was slacked off, and the dazed and half-strangled yearling staggered to his feet. For a full minute he stood gasping, the muddy sweat streaming from his heaving sides.

Then, as his lungs filled and the numbness passed from his brain, a dull, crimson light glowed deep in his great eyes. They looked as Bald Stockings' eyes had looked when she killed the wolf. With a snort like a pistol shot he bounded to escape. Two Leggings and Standing Bear on the halter rope, Iron Horse and two others on the tail rope, bucking, kicking, squealing, he dragged them around the dusty corral. It couldn't last—eight hundred and fifty pounds of wiry Crow to be dragged by a colt who weighed little more. Three times the pinto tried it, and three times the Indians dragged him to a stop. By that time his head was bleeding where the rough rope halter cut into the tender skin behind his ears and around his nose and jaw. When the third rush was over and before the colt had begun to recover from the struggle, leaving the other three to man the ropes, Two Leggings and Iron Horse mounted their ponies. Two Leggings going ahead with the halter rope, Iron Horse behind with the tail rope, an Indian on each side of the captured colt to flog him and keep him straight, they half dragged, half drove him from the corral. The other colt dashed past him through the gate, and the remaining Indian, Two Toes, (he had lost half his right foot in a bear trap), stayed behind to turn loose the horses when captors and captive should have disappeared.

The last shafts of sunlight were glinting on the shallows of the Yellowstone when the hot and tired procession reached the river. Half way across the ford, where the water was knee deep, the Indians stopped to let their thirsty ponies drink. Two Leggings' buckskin sank his muzzle to the eyes and Two Leggings leaned down to scoop a handful of water for himself. As he slacked the head-rope for a moment, some instinct of self-preservation stirred the pinto colt. He bounded up stream, jerking Two Leggings and Iron Horse into the water. He gained the bank three lengths ahead of the flank Indians. In a breath the three lengths had spun to ten; the colt was free, and the cursing Indians, though they used their heavy quirts at every bound, knew they could no more catch him than they could catch the cloud-shadows that sail across the plains. Ten lengths, twenty lengths, and then the pinto turned a somersault, and lay still. He had stepped on the trailing head-rope, and the chase was done.

Before the colt recovered himself enough to stand, the dripping Two Leggings and Iron Horse came up and manned the ropes. In less time than it takes to tell it, the dreary procession was on its way again, and this time the river was crossed without incident. The ponies and Indians drank their fill, but the pinto yearling was too sick in mind and body even to try. He spent that night many miles to the south in a tiny corral, near where a wandering streamlet from the foothills trickles into the Little Horn, while Two Leggings and his three wives slept nearby under the battered hearse, and the other Indians curled up along the fence.

The Indian ponies had been staggering with fatigue when they reached camp the night before, but there is no other breed of horse that with feed and water can so quickly recover from hard use as an Indian pony in his native environment; and next morning, before the first rose had tinted the top of Pompey's Pillar, they were ready, as fit for another day as a stabled horse after an hour in the park.

Pinto snorted when Two Leggings entered the corral, and backed away as far as he could, which was just what Two Leggings wanted, for it let him reach the trailing head and tail ropes which had not been taken off. Again there came the same unequal struggle as there had been the afternoon before in the home corral, but the colt was sore and tired and empty, and it did not take as long to stretch him helpless. Some time before, Mrs. Two Leggings and the other ladies had built a fire near the gate, and now she handed Two Leggings a long piece of smooth heavy wire, looped at one end—the loop end red hot. Two Leggings stepped between the yearling's stretched legs, and with care applied the heated loop to the colt's quarter, half way between the hip and hock. The hiss of burning flesh was lost in Two Leggings' yell, for as the pinto felt the sting, his snake-like head shot back and his teeth sank deep in the Indian's scrawny calf. That did not do any good either; his hold was broken by the butt of Iron Horse's quirt which nearly broke his nose, and while this happened, the red hot wire which Two Leggings had dropped, slowly burned a furrow across the black patch on the colt's shoulder.

Two Leggings carried the marks of those white teeth always, and one of the young ladies, who had the bad taste to laugh, was soundly thumped by Mrs. Two Leggings, with the neck-yoke. When order was restored, the wire re-heated and the pinto's head tied down, Two Leggings limped up, and, slowly and with care, drew a rough picture of a crow on the colt's quarter, while the colt, his eyes closed now, shriveled in helpless agony. The rest he only remembered as a burning night-mare. All day, while the Montana sun beat down on the treeless plains, the Indians half led, half dragged him across the ridges that divided the Little Big Horn from the Lodge Grass, and not until long after the last light had faded over the Big Horns, and they had reached a meadow where the Lodge Grass swings out from the foot-hills, did they stop to camp.

That night, while the battered colt dozed in the corner of a pole corral, Patch Hinton opened the Ball over the general store at Billings with Miss Tessie Buckland, (formerly of somewhat light character) now one of Butte's best known and most respected citizens. Miss Buckland had once done the Bishop a favor in the matter of a nephew, some blue chips, much "Red Eye," and a fair-haired stranger. The Bishop would as soon have missed his call on her on his semi-annual trip through the Diocese, as he would his call on the District Judge or the President of the Bank; and, even if Miss Buckland was not invited to take tea at the rector's or to play whist with the banker's wife, she had a warm friend in the rector, who knew he could count on her heart and her purse in any emergency; and an equally warm one in the banker, who sometimes advised her as to her investments, but more often asked her advice about people in whom he had a political or financial interest. She knew every one of consequence in that part of Montana, and there was very little that went on, reputable or otherwise, that escaped her. What she did not know about men and horses you could put in a flea's ear.

She came each year to the Billings Fair to exchange, for a time, the banal and sophisticated pleasantries of the mining gentry for the more impulsive and original atmosphere of the gentlemen of the Plains. She rode a crop-eared roan gelding, considered the best saddle horse in three states. Usually, she opened the Ball with the mayor, if unmarried; but this mayor was married and was also in bed with a gun-shot wound in his thigh; so Mr. Hinton, dean of Yellowstone County bachelors, held the Ace.

Edward Borein

CHAPTER V

In the spring of the year that the Indians stole Pinto, old Lord Palmadime, father of the Honorable William Spencer Fitzhenry Wantage, concluded, in his wisdom, that his eldest son, Lord Ernest, should make a visit to his younger brother to study The States, against the time when he would succeed to the House of Lords and the responsibility of guiding the destinies of an empire. Queer place, The States. But they seemed to keep on growing and becoming more important in spite of the Americans' shockin' manners and loud voices, and certainly they did produce some very attractive and rich women. Yes, Ernest should go over (he was very presentable). So that summer, Lord Ernest went to study The States. He spent a week playing polo at Westchester, another at Newport dining out, and then went to Wyoming. He introduced the cowboys to polo, which they took to gaily; and ranch work vanished as they schooled ponies and planned a match at the Sheridan Fair with the Moncrieffe team from Big Horn.

Lord Ernest read them "Ivanhoe" in the evenings, and so enchanted were they with the tournament at Ashby de la Zouche that they had to have one of their own. They cut the ends out of peach baskets and covered the holes with chicken wire, for helmets. For lances they cut long poles and nailed a board over the head end, for they had no armor to turn a thrust. Slim Williams and Texas Siftings were drawn for the first Joust—the lists, a dusty lane down which they spurred their ponies from fifty yards apart. Truly they met, and gallantly their thrusts went home—knights and horses bit the dust. Sir Slim "got" Sir Siftings in the face, mashed his nose and drove the chicken wire in. Sir

Siftings landed on Sir Slim's middle and tore away three ribs; one pierced a lung. That ended Jousting, and the Moncrieffe Match; for two of the team were hauled to town for repairs, instead of polo.

Then that particular study of The States being finished, the Honorable Wantage decided that he would make his Fall inspection of the Bull Mountain horses early, so that Lord Ernest could see them and still get home in time for the Opening Meet at Palmadime. En route, he would show Lord Ernest a different kind of hunting, for in those days the Big Horns were full of game—black-tail in the lower country, elk in the higher parks, and sheep above the timber line about Cloud Peak.

A few days after the Indians and Pinto arrived at the Lodge Grass camp, the hunting party, with many heads, found itself at the end of the mountains, where they had to descend to the plains for the rest of the journey. The pack outfit was sent straight down the trail; the Honorable and Lord Ernest cut across the lower parks, hoping for another shot at a black-tail. They would meet the outfit that evening to camp in the lower country. They rode with care, but saw no game and ate their lunch on the last high spur where they could look out over the plains. Thirty miles to the north, they could see a fringe of yellow that marked the bluffs on the far side of the Yellowstone, while in front, the brown expanse was unrelieved, except where lines of green showed the course of the Big Horn, the Little Big Horn, and the lesser streams.

By three o'clock, well down in the lower country, they came on an Indian camp, a battered hearse parked in the alders, and a whinneying pinto yearling in a pole corral. They rode up to look, and the colt pawed at the gate. Wantage marked at once the rope burns and the recent brand, but Lord Ernest thought only of buying the colt, and when the Indians strolled up, Wantage asked by signs if they would sell. Twenty dollars? No! Thirty dollars? No!

Forty dollars? No! That was strange—you could buy any horse on the reservation for fifteen dollars. The old squaw suddenly pointed to the brand on the Wantage horses, and jabbered to Iron Horse. The Honorable whistled "The Spanish Cavalier"—the colt tried to climb the fence.

The Honorable wrote a note and Lord Ernest cantered off down the creek with it. Lord Ernest would find and bring the outfit up. The note was to the Indian Agent. One of the horse wranglers would take it to the Agency, and the Agent would come out next day. The Honorable climbed up and sat on the gate. The Indians went back to the bushes and talked much. The colt crowded as near the gate as he could and switched flies, which settled on the fresh scars, while the Honorable rolled a cigarette. At four, he saw the two bucks loping away over a ridge to the south. At four-thirty, the tepee was down and packed and the hearse was jingling off in the same direction, the old squaw on the box, the younger ladies, free now from the watchful eye of their owner, as outside passengers. In an hour more, the outfit and Lord Ernest appeared, and the next morning, with the colt in tow, they started for the Agency. Half way there, they met the Agent and Patch.

It had happened this way: the colt had been stolen by the Indians on Monday. On Friday, late in the afternoon, Patch and his mules came jogging home from the Fair. Not far from where the road to Hinton's cabin leaves the Yellowstone stage road, he saw the band of horses. He drove over to count them, and straightway missed the pinto yearling. That was queer! Patch straightened up on the seat, and the mules mended their pace as they were turned back to the road. Perhaps for some reason, Weston had kept the colt up. Perhaps he was now lying injured somewhere on the range. There was not much that could happen to him at this season. The wolves did not bother the horses in summer, and the bog holes were dried up. He might have broken his leg in a prairie-dog hole, or been knocked over and trampled by the other horses in some sudden rush. Anyway, it must be seen to "pronto", and the off mule got a harder crack than when Patch had thought of the biscuit-shooter.

Ten minutes later, where the road crosses the Cottonwood, the off-mule snorted and jumped sideways against his mate, with every sign of fear. Patch could neither see nor smell anything unusual, and getting up on the level again out of the creek bottom, the mules calmed down. The slightest eddy of wind had come down the draw, carrying the taint of the Indian camp which had been in a grove of trees fifty yards upstream. Patch drove to the cabin and Weston walked out to meet him. The story was quickly told. When Bill had come over on Wednesday to count the horses, the tracks of the Indians' moccasins and the struggle in the corral were written plain in the dust. Patch knew that pursuit was useless. He knew enough about the Indians to feel sure that they would hide the pinto colt in some out of the way hiding place on the reservation. He knew that, alone, he might as well look for the diamond he had lost from his shirt-front two years before when the mules had tipped him over in the river. The Indians would know where he was all the time, and move the colt in the night to new hiding places. With flashes from a piece of mirror, or with smoke signals by day, and with a camp fire alternately blanketed and shown by night, the Indians could talk across the plains as the telegraph talks on its wire. No, a lone hunt was no good. He must notify the agent, and then wait for results.

Next morning, leaving Slippery Bill the double duty of keeping tab on both herds, he took his best saddle-horse and started south. Late in the afternoon of the next day he was tying his pony to the rail in front of the Agency, when he noticed, tied near him, a horse with the Wantage brand, and five minutes later, he was reading the note that the Honorable William Spencer Fitzhenry had written to the Agent. Next day, when the Agent and Patch met the Englishmen with their pack outfit and the pinto, the Agent made no difficulty in acknowledging that Hinton owned the colt. When the party reached the home corrals on Big Coulee, the colt was put into the squeeze, (two fences which could be pulled together by a lever to hold a horse for branding, and do away with the struggle and fright of being roped and thrown); the Crow brand was vented, that is a straight bar was branded through it, making it void, and the colt, still sore and thin from his hard experience, was turned in with the saddle horses.

MISS TESSIE BUCKLAND (PAGE 24)

CHAPTER VI

The Honorable Wantage and Lord Ernest stayed to help Patch pick out from the broken geldings the twenty head of half-breds that Patch was to take to England to make into hunters. A week later, when he started with them for the railroad, the winter regime at Big Coulee began again with the double band of brood mares turned on their winter range in the hills—the pinto colt with the saddle horses, and Slippery Bill Weston left in charge.

December, January and February went by without incident. It was the hardest winter since '86, but the brood mares could always find good grass and shelter in the pine-protected parks; and the saddle horses, with whom Pinto lived, had an ample supply of blue-stem hay when the snow lay too deep on the open hillsides.

One morning, it must have been early March, for the days had begun to lengthen, though the cold was still bitter and the snow lay deep, the impatient geldings crowding around the hay corral, saw no smoke come from the cabin chimney, and Weston never came to fill the hay racks. Until noon they waited sourly, and then, driven by hunger, trooped out through the drifts to scrape through the snow where it lay thinnest on the ridges, for what grass they could find. At dusk they came straggling back, half satisfied, to find Jennie, the range heifer, which Patch as a great luxury had caught and taught to be milked, lowing mournfully at the corral gate. She lived in the hay corral with the saddle horses; but there was no hay, no one to feed and milk her, her udder was aching and she did not know enough to dig through the snow for feed as the horses did. That night the worst blizzard of the year broke from the North. The second morning there was no sunlight, only a dull greyness, filled with swirling snow, and the forty mile gale from Hudson Bay made the stout corral fence sway like a sweet-pea trellis in a summer breeze. There was no going out that day; even the tough old geldings could not stand against the storm. No one came, and the only sound in the intervals of the increasing gale was the heifer's moaning call.

That night the cold grew more bitter; a thermometer would have registered forty degrees below zero. The third morning, all that remained of the cow was a higher drift near the gate. That morning, some of the older horses tried for the open, but staggered back after going fifty yards, beaten by the wind and the drifts. For four days the Storm God rode the range, and the stronger horses, maddened now by hunger and cold, fought each other like wolves for even the little protection of the corral fence.

Pinto was the youngest and weakest, and was pushed to the outside of the huddled horses, where the warmth and protection from the others was slightest. He was failing fast—another twenty-four hours and he would join the cow. He stood braced to the storm, his legs apart, his head touching the drift, too dulled by cold and hunger even to try any longer for a warmer spot. It had all happened before in the Northwest; animals caught in a storm against a fence, or pocketed in a canyon, had frozen as they stood. Patch Hinton could have told you that in the spring of '87 he had walked for a full mile up a canyon on the Box Elder, stepping from carcass to carcass. These had been twelve thousand head of southern two-year-old steers which he and his father had turned loose on the Bull Mountain Range in the fall of '86. Of the twelve thousand, they gathered seventy-five head in the spring round-up.

Among the older gelding was a flea-bitten, much branded grey savage that had come up from Texas with a trail-herd years before. He was goose-rumped and fiddle-headed, he was a sink of wickedness and a well of wisdom; he was up to every trick of the range. If he could not gain what he wanted from the other horses by stealth or bluff, he would fight like a wildcat. He could slash another horse's neck with his teeth and then kick him cunningly in the groin before the other horse knew a fight had started. He could seize another's ear and shake him until he screamed. Of a morning in the corral, he could dodge Patch's rope until even that polished swearer choked. But once let the rope settle over that scarred, gray head and no lady's lap-dog followed its leash more gently. He was the ace of the cavvy (meaning saddle-horse herd, from the Spanish "caballo" meaning horse). Hinton always rode him on his hardest rides; he knew that when the end of that savage strength seemed at hand, there was always one more effort in the whalebone frame, and one more wish to arrive in that wicked head. With Patch, the gray horse tried no tricks; he recognized a master's hand; but let a newcomer try to ride him! (It was whispered among the other horses that once, years before, he had thrown a man on Tongue River and then had kneeled and savaged him). Lord Ernest tried to ride him against Patch's advice; but, fine horseman though he was, he had been bucked so high that Patch, telling of it afterwards, said that a swallow came along and built a nest in his hat before he came down!

Now the old gelding, gaunt as a winter wolf, his long hair matted with the driving snow, stood hunched against the gate, the warmest place there was. A lumpish, brown horse that had come up from Nebraska with some surveyors, so stupid with cold and hunger that he forgot himself, pushed in between the Texas savage and the gate, determined to gain even that small shelter at any cost. Like a streak of lightning in the dark, the gray horse came to life, whirling off his hocks, and without a sound, he seized the other's ear and with one leg across the brown's withers shook his larger opponent as a game terrier shakes a badger half again his size. The brown horse, floundering to escape, fell against the gate, which flew open with a squeetch, as the staple which held the hook was pulled from the post, and both horses rolled into the main corral out of sight in a smother of snow. The other horses, too numb to know what the open gate meant, stood staring stupidly. Not so the grizzled gray; he dropped the brown horse as if he were hot, and struggled to his feet with a wild neigh of relief, for he knew that the open gate meant freedom, and freedom meant access to the pine-clad hills, if he had strength enough left to win through the intervening drifts. The gray's wild call roused the others, and they surged through the gate, the pinto yearling staggering in their wake.

CHAPTER VII

A month later, Patch Hinton, returning from abroad, landed at the end of the railroad, got his saddle and bridle from the livery barn, his horse from a neighboring ranch, and on a sunny, windswept April afternoon arrived at his cabin at the big corral. There was not a sign of life. The starved frame of old Thomas, the black and white cat, lay stretched on the doorstep. He opened the door, and a rat scuttled across the floor. There in his bunk he found what was left of Bill Weston. He had died as he slept, so suddenly that not even the blankets were disturbed.

Patch went for his pick and spade, and near the gate of the hay corral, found the bones of Jennie, picked and scattered by the wolves. The tragedy of that lonely winter was written clear. After Weston was buried and stones piled high on his grave to keep the coyotes from digging into it, Patch, a coffee-pot and frying pan on his saddle, again mounted his horse to look for his band of horses in the hills, determined to camp in the open, away from a place where the breath of death seemed still to hang. Just at dusk, a mile higher up the valley, he shot a blacktail buck, and there he camped, dozing through the night, his back against a cottonwood, rousing himself from time to time to keep his fire going; for he had no blankets, and April nights in that high country are cold.

Next morning, before the stars had faded, he hung the buck high in a tree, out of reach of prowling coyotes, and before the day was two hours old he came upon the first of the saddle horses. By twos and threes, he found them scattered over a mile of timbered hillside. All were there, none the worse now for

TRULY THEY MET, AND GALLANTLY THEIR THRUSTS WENT HOME (PAGE 27)

their terrible experience in the blizzard except the pinto two-year-old, whose thin neck and creased quarters showed that he had suffered more than his older and hardier companions, but he trotted gaily to meet Patch when he whistled "The Spanish Cavalier" and Patch knew that a month on the new spring grass would bring him back. Three miles farther along the hills he began to find the mares. Two head were missing—an oldish chestnut mare that had been knocked down and injured the autumn before, and the brown Stowaway two-year-old, that had fought the pinto in the spring. The mare, he never saw again; the colt, he later found dead in a bog-hole into which he had foolishly ventured. As soon as Patch had counted the mares, he hurried back to the saddle horses, rounded them up, and drove them to the home corral, the Texas Ruffian leading the band, after first having tried to slip off unnoticed down a timbered draw. He picked up the buck on the way; he knew that except for the coffee, the pack rats and chipmunks had ruined the provisions at the cabin. Once in the main corral, the mules were roped and the rest of the band turned into the saddle horse pasture, for Patch must hurry to Billings for supplies and to hire someone to take Weston's place for the summer's work. That afternoon he started, and the next morning the mules ate breakfast in Ed Taintor's livery barn, and Patch had "ham and" at the Grand Hotel.

Twenty-four hours later he was starting back. The wagon was now loaded, and there were two men on the seat, a saddled pony trotting behind. For Patch had found the very man he might have prayed for—"Chips" Aubrey, born within a mile of where Patch was raised, on the banks of the Brazos, in Southern Texas. The boys had grown up together, had hired out together for their first job, come north with a trail-herd, and, always inseparable, had punched cows together for fifteen years from the Little Missouri to the Panhandle, from the Nebraska sandhills to the

Big Bend in Oregon. They treated horses alike, and Hinton knew if he searched the whole West he could find no one who would work with him as Aubrey would. After his winter in England, Patch realized that if the hunter prospects from the Bull Mountain herd could be given a preliminary schooling over fences, an infinite amount of time and trouble, which meant expense, would be saved when he took the next lot to the other side.

He had hired another man he knew to look after the mares that ranged on the Mussel Shell, and three weeks after they had reached the home camp, and before the Honorable Wantage arrived with the stallions, and the mares had been turned out on the summer range, a round corral was built of lodge-pole pine, big enough to school several horses at once. Ditches were dug, some on one side and some on the other of the pole jumps, and after the Honorable had come, and the summer regime was established, the work of breaking and schooling the young hunters started in earnest. It was fine material to work with; those well-bred, range-bred horses, active as cats, accustomed to look after themselves, and to jump the dry arroyas from the time that they were foals. After the first few days' hesitation at the strange obstacles, they would sail away over six feet of ditch and four feet of poles as a jack-rabbit sails the sage; and Pinto, who always came with them when they were driven in from the pasture, took his turn with the rest; until at the end of a month, discovering that it was as easy to jump wire as it was the pole jumps, he jumped in and out of the pasture as he pleased, spending now a few days with the brood mares, and then turning up some morning with the saddle horses. Patch feared he would teach the older horses to jump wire, and then there would be no controlling them, but he did not realize that they had not begun their schooling early enough, and that they would never overcome the respect for wire learned by sharp experience as they were growing up.

One morning, just at daybreak, Pinto was grazing with his friends in the saddle horse pasture, half a mile from where the north fence runs along the foot of a yellow bluff. A yearling wolf, returning to his den in the hills after a night hunting rabbits in the open country, trotted by a hundred yards in front of the horses. He was up wind, and the pinto threw up his head with a snort. The wolf stopped and looked, surprised to see the black and white horse leave the others like a bullet. It never occurred to him that the black and white streak was coming after him; no horse ever chased a wolf except at close quarters, and moreover, there was a wide wash between dug deep by the spring rains. Curiosity overcame him; the paint horse was clearly loco, crazy from eating loco weed; he'd either fall into the ditch and break his silly neck and provide a good meal for some days, or stop when he got to it. But the paint horse skimmed the gulch as a swallow skims a pond, and the young wolf, now thoroughly frightened, made for the fence. He slipped through, fifty yards ahead of the horse; but the gasp of relief choked in his throat, and the hair along his back stood up in terror, for the paint horse, scarcely checking his stride, jumped the fence. For sixty yards, the ground rose gently to the foot of the bluff, and up this slope wolf and horse were now racing, the wolf to save his life, the horse to take it.

A coyote, about to bed down for the day on the brow of the yellow bluff, had watched the whole scene, and shivering with excitement as the horse gained on his prey, yelled to the wolf to dodge; but the young wolf, too terror-stricken to listen, kept straight on. Twenty yards from the hill, when the black spot on the pinto's shoulder was even with the wolf's hips, his head went down with a vicious sideways lunge, and the wolf shot ten feet in the air, while the pinto plunged to a stop in a spatter of sand and broken sage. Before the wolf, half stunned by the twisting fall, could gain his feet, the horse was on him. A lucky blow from a black fore-foot broke his lower jaw, and the watching coyote, through the swirling dust, could see the pinto strike and stamp his adversary until no sign of life remained. Then the pinto shook the battered body as he'd seen his mother do, until with a final vicious toss he threw it to one side, trotted down the slope and popped over the fence to join the other horses, which had trotted after him curiously, until the wires blocked their path.

Now the coyotes are the gossips of the range, and every night they yap and yell to the world all that they have seen and heard in the last twenty-four hours. That night all the range for ten miles heard what had happened, and although the young wolf's mother rumbled in her throat something about the pack and next winter, the story spread until every wolf and coyote travelled that part of the country with one eye peeled for the pinto horse, and if, for some reason, they had to pass near him, they were careful to do so down wind and with the rise of a hill between. Even old Lobo, the acknowledged leader of all the wolves from the Madison to the Rosebud, carelessly showing himself on the skyline near where Pinto was feeding with the mares, was chased ignominiously three miles up the Cottonwood bottoms and got away only by dodging into an alder thicket. Perhaps it was just as well that Pinto didn't catch up with him, for he was still only a baby and old Lobo could pull down a four-year-old steer alone.

CHAPTER VIII

That summer passed pleasantly for Pinto. He divided his time between the brood-mares and the saddle horses, coming and going as he pleased, while Hinton and Chips went on with the business of breaking and schooling the young horses. June had become July, the plains' carpet of wild flowers had come and gone, the Gentian and the Paint-Brush in the upper meadows sparkled in the brilliant August mornings, when one day, just as Patch and Chips had finished their midday snack, a man and woman in a light spring wagon drove up to the cabin at Big Coulee. The man, small, thin and wiry, sat on the extreme end of the seat, one leg hanging over the side, for the billowing proportions of his companion left him little room.

Patch knew them at once. The man might have passed anywhere unnoticed, but that ample figure in the blue calico dress could never be mistaken, though the huge sunbonnet hid the jolly face. It was Mr. and Mrs. Billy Clark. They had worked for a season for the Honorable on the Powder River Ranch some years ago, before the Bull Mountain outfit was started. Patch knew that Clark knew more about bitting and mannering saddle horses than anyone in the cow country, and Mrs. Clark had a reputation as a cook as far east as the Nebraska line; and he knew that, when the big woman smiled, every dog on the place wagged his tail and every human laughed and felt as if he were on a vacation in California.

Clark was English born, and until he was twenty-one had spent his life making hunters for his father, who at that time, kept the principal job-master's establishment at Melton. Subsequently, he had come to America with a consignment of hunters, had worked for five years as assistant in the trained-horse department of Barnum and Bailey's Circus, until meeting Mrs. Clark in Cheyenne, he had married and settled on a homestead on the Belle Fourche, in Southern Wyoming. Here things went well for a time, and he had gradually accumulated a small band of horses and cattle, when the terrible winter of '86 and '87 wiped him out, as it had so many ranchers, large and small, and he had had to go to work as a common hand.

Hinton realized that Clark had forgotten more about making hunters than he would ever know, and he hugged himself with pleasure, for it looked as if the Clarks had come to stay. In the back of the spring wagon was a horse-hide trunk, tied with rope, a tent, a bed-roll, a cooking outfit, a large coop full of Plymouth-Rocks, and tied on top of the coop a rusty parrot cage in which sat solemnly the biggest Maltese cat that Patch had ever seen.

Explanation was quickly made. Clark, breaking colts on the "Y Cross" on the upper Madison, had heard from a traveling stranger who stopped for the night, of the crazy cowboys and the jumping horses at Big Coulee, and, recognizing the Wantage brand from the stranger's description, knew that the Honorable must be trying the experiment he used to talk about at Powder River. He saw a chance to get a steady job at the work he liked best, and straightway he and Mrs. Clark had loaded their possessions in the spring-wagon and had come down to see for themselves. In an hour the tent was pitched on the creek bank, fifty yards from the cabin, the Plymouth Rocks were scratching contentedly nearby, the Clark horses were munching hay in the corral, and Jumbo, the Maltese cat, was catching his first Big Coulee rat in the storehouse. From appearances, they might have been there for a month, but Hinton, when he came in for supper, hugged himself again, for the untidy litter of the man-kept cabin was gone and he and Chips had a meal the like of which they hadn't thought of since they were last in town.

Pinto had not been on hand when the newcomers arrived. He had never seen a white woman, and next morning, coming around the corner of the house for his usual piece of bread at breakfast time, he met, face to face, the great blue figure, all flapping in the morning breeze. He had been frightened when the Indians caught him, but he had been helpless then; now he was free. Without taking time to snort, he ducked back around the corner of the house, and raced away five miles to where the mares were grazing, at such a pace that old Mule-Ears, the head jackrabbit of those parts, blinked with envy where he sat dozing in the shadow of a sage. But the blue thing, whatever it was, had not followed him, and two mornings later Pinto came up to the corrals when Chips drove in the saddle horses.

By degrees, he learned that the blue thing was like his other human friends; in fact, even more to be depended on for odd pieces of bread during the day. The chickens, at first, puzzled him, too, and Hinton had to give him two or three severe lessons before he learned that Jumbo was not to be hunted on sight, like the coyotes. He found in Clark, who from the first look recognized the colt's out-standing class, as great an ally as Patch. At odd moments as the summer waned, Clark taught him many tricks, so that when the Honorable came in October on his regular round, he would lie down at a signal and play dead from as far away as he could see his teacher; he would stand or lie stock still and allow Hinton or Clark to use him as a rest for their heavy rifles, and he could fill and carry a bucket of water, with the handle in his teeth, from the spring to the cabin and scarcely spill a drop.

Before Patch left with the horses for England that autumn, a cabin was built for the Clarks, and that winter being a mild

A MAN AND WOMAN IN A LIGHT SPRING WAGON DROVE UP TO THE CABIN (PAGE 43)

one, the pinto thrived and grew, but he was never allowed to forget any of the lessons that he had learned, and by the time that Patch came back in the spring, Clark was riding the big three-year-old regularly. He taught him to back indefinitely and practiced him at it much, to supple the muscles of his neck and strengthen his back and loins. He taught him to carry a light-curb bit with comfort; and although he was seldom ridden outside the main corral, and never at speed, Pinto learned to respond to the slightest pressure of rein or heel. Hinton never rode him for he weighed, with his heavy California saddle, nearly two hundred pounds, and so the work of mannering was left to Clark, who, with a light English saddle which Lord Ernest had sent out, scarcely weighed one hundred and fifty.

By July, the colt was taking Clark for the mail twice a week, and gradually, as Clark realized more and more how rapidly he was developing with the regular exercise, he began to think what a fine thing it would be to take the colt to the Billings Fair. Finally, he broached the question to Patch, who promptly turned it down. But Clark was persistent, and finally persuaded Patch that it was almost necessary to bring the colt, while still young, into contact with the outside world, lest so active and high-strung an animal, if allowed to go too long without knowing anything but the range, might never become accustomed to other conditions. That was the excuse for taking him, but Patch and Clark knew, though it was never mentioned, that the real reason for taking him was to give them a chance to show off their jewel. And so Hinton and Mr. and Mrs. Clark and Pinto went to the Fair; the Clarks in the spring wagon, Hinton on a quiet horse, leading Pinto, until they reached the edge of town, when Clark got down and led him on foot. For Pinto, with his confidence in man, was always quieter being led on foot than beside another horse. The following morning, Clark led the restless colt, for two hours, up and down the Billings streets and out to the fair-grounds, letting him stop to smell of everything; and the colt, finding that the novel sights and sounds and smells did him no harm, by noon would go anywhere with scarcely a snort or shy.

That afternoon when the races and contests were to start, Hinton, on his quiet horse, and Clark on Pinto, rode to the fair-grounds. Patch, who generally acted as one of the marshals, got Clark and the pinto into the in-field. There they watched the roping contests, the wild-horse race, the bucking horses, and all the hair-raising events of an old-fashioned frontier exhibition of the cowboy's art. Hinton and Clark were having a good time; for the pinto, in the morning, had attracted more attention than any horse that had ever been in Billings, and Patch had had many offers for him—from old Square Tail's two oldest daughters to the thousand dollars gold which Miss Buckland offered the minute she saw him being led by the hotel. The colt had become quiet enough by the middle of the afternoon, so that Clark and Hinton thought, or each said to the other that he thought, it would be a fine thing to take him through the quarter stretch and past the grandstand, to accustom him to the crowd. So, in the lull between the wild-horse race and the bucking contest, they rode down the track, Patch on the quiet horse on the rail, Clark on the pinto next the grandstand. Patch noticed that the pinto was sweating a little, and he whispered to Clark to "mind his eye."

In those days, in Montana, everyone depended on horses for their livelihood and often for their lives. The horse was king, and as the pinto, his black and white coat hand-rubbed until Clark's arms ached, stepped nervously down the stretch, a ripple of applause broke along the grandstand, and the leader of the band, from his place in the center, thinking to add something, he didn't know exactly what, rose suddenly with his baton, and the band broke out with a blare. With a bound like a panther's, Pinto was over the rail and tearing across the in-field, Clark sitting back and for a second or two fighting for control. The hazers posted about the track and in-field to keep the bucking horses away from the fences, spurred to head him off, but they might just as well have spurred to head off a plains antelope. He flipped in and out over the low rail fences on the far side of the track, and then Clark caught his breath; the colt was flying across the short stretch of dusty turf, straight for the board fence that rimmed the grounds. It was four feet ten of rough-sawed plank, without a break in it on that side, and although Clark knew that Pinto could jump, it was one thing to jump four feet quietly with no weight up; it was going up a different street to jump nearly five with a hundred and fifty pounds up, and at that terror-driven pace. But he saw that he was in for it. He dropped his hands, and still as a statue he sat, leaning a little forward. Three lengths from the fence the colt's ears went up, and eight feet from it he took off and went up and over it as a driven pheasant rockets over a high line of trees. He landed on the sun-baked county road with a jolt that split Clark's lip against his neck, and snapping himself together, set off down the road as hard as ever. It took Clark two miles to stop him, and he led the blown, but still nervous, colt back a quarter of a mile before he met Patch with Miss Buckland and some other friends galloping to meet him. They returned to town, Patch leading the pinto, with Clark riding double on Miss Buckland's roan; and Patch gave strict orders that the colt was not to be taken near the fair-grounds again.

That evening around the Billings streets, there was much talk about the pinto colt and Clark's ride; and Al Honeydew, the Butte gambler, offered to bet one thousand dollars to five hundred that there wasn't another horse at the Fair that could

ODD PIECES OF BREAD DURING THE DAY (PAGE 45)

go out over the back fence without a fall. Clark was standing at the bar of Ben Prim's Place, and much talk was flowing about the colt's burst of speed, when a wizened man, in a battered derby, standing three places down the bar from Clark, remarked that no half-bred could gallop with a clean-bred of any class. Now it had been agreed between Clark and Hinton before they left home, that on no account should the pinto be galloped in company, much less raced; but Clark had taken about three fingers two much well-seasoned Rye, and three fingers too much well-seasoned Rye is contentious stuff. Before he realized what he was doing, he had bet the stranger five hundred dollars that the pinto could beat any horse half a mile that he might show. The stranger answered not but handed over five hundred dollars to the bar-keep, and then Clark knew he was hooked. He did not have five hundred dollars to his name, and Hinton must be found. He found him playing a quiet game of draw with Miss Buckland and a few friends in the back parlor of the Grand Hotel. It was a mad, but silent, Patch that went back with him to the saloon, paid his five hundred dollars to the stake-holding bar-keep and matched for the choice of start and lost. The wizened stranger chose a standing start; and Patch's worst fear was confirmed when he went back to the hotel, for Miss Buckland promptly named the man, and said he owned a brown horse that had cleaned up the country around Butte the spring before.

The race, not being part of the regular program, was set for eleven in the morning, and so rapidly had the talk of it spread through the town, that at ten-thirty, there were nearly as many people in the grandstand as there had been the afternoon before. It was catch weights, and although Clark could make no less than one hundred and forty-five pounds, Patch was afraid to risk a stranger on the colt which, still nervous from his previous fright, was being walked about the in-field. At ten-fifty-five, the wizened man led in a brown gelding, half a hand smaller than Pinto, old-looking but sound, with the lean, game head of a thoroughbred and all the marks of what once must have been a horse of real class. A slip of a darkey rode him; he had the best of the weight by forty pounds, and the wizened man was offering two to one, with no takers.

The President of the Fair was to be starter and judge. It was a half-mile track and the horses were to break at the tap of the big drum in the center of the grandstand. Patch told the president that Clark was a little deaf and to hit the drum hard. They tossed for places; Hinton won and took the outside. They lined up, and twice the brown horse broke before the drum sounded, while the pinto, remembering his scare of the previous afternoon, stood still, shaking, one eye on the grandstand, with half a mind to bolt as he had before. Crash! went the drum. The brown horse broke like a summer storm, and the crowd in the grandstand rose with a yell; for the "paint" horse broke with him, and stride for stride, he held him as they swept around the first turn. Into the back stretch they went, locked level, and the colored boy, surprised and frightened now, sat down to ride. Patch's stratagem had worked; for the drum crash had terrified the green colt into a flying start, and his outside place kept the brown horse between him and the rail. But the drum's crash wasn't followed by anything awful, and the colt began to ease up and wonder what it all meant. One length, two lengths, three lengths, the brown slipped ahead, and although the pinto was still galloping fast, his head and ears were up and he played with his snaffle bit.

Those were the longest seconds that Clark ever passed. He dared not hit the colt; he could only sit still and wait, and pray that some instinct would wake in the colt's brain and tell him to race. Ten lengths from the far turn, the pinto's wandering eye caught the flying brown. What did that gollumping brown camel think he was doing out there in front? Some sand which stung, hit him in the face; and the crowd in the grandstand, which had sunk back into apathy, jumped to its feet again with a yell that was heard in town; for the pinto head went out and the pinto ears came back, and the blood of a thousand racing ancestors went through his veins like flame, as the pinto began to run. Into the straight they swung, and the three lengths had been cut to two. Clark, stretched out along the colt's neck, thought—if only the crowd would not yell so and wave their hats; and some damn fool was beating the drum! But the pinto heard nothing now. He only saw the brown quarters driving on in front. Clark didn't realize the kind of horse he was riding; he needn't have worried; nothing short of a bullet could have stopped him. On he swept, and now only a length separated the black-and-white muzzle from the brown's tail. Nearer he crept, and nearer. The pinto horse was running as he had never run before; and when they came to the end of the grandstand, the scar on his black shoulder lapped the brown's hips. There for a breath he hung, for the game brown horse made a final drive. Then his tail went up, and the "paint" horse shot under the wire a half length to the good. He never stopped until he missed the brown on the back stretch, and then Clark slipped off him, and without waiting even for Patch, led him straight to the barn.

That afternoon Ed Taintor's barn was crowded, and Patch soon found that he had to shut the doors against the crowd. The colt, nearly frantic with excitement, would neither eat nor drink, but walked his stall like a new-caught wolf. So fearful were the two men lest he do himself an injury, that they decided to take him home; and the next morning, before the crowd was stirring, the Bull Mountain outfit left.

EDWARD BOREIN

CHAPTER IX

In every band of horses that have run together for any length of time, a line of precedence becomes established—a precedence as clearly marked among horses as it is among the diplomats of London or Paris. What the characteristics are that establish this precedence is not always clear—age, experience, strength, fighting ability, cunning, perhaps a balanced average of all. But anyone who will observe a strange horse turned in with a crew of horses that have run together for some time, will notice that in a comparatively few days the stranger will have found his level, often with no open fighting. There is some way in which horses can take each other's measure without actual conflict; and once that measure is established, unless man or some unusual incident upsets it, you will find that in the case of horses running undisturbed it is seldom broken.

Pinto was the youngest among the saddle horses, and his place in the line of precedence had always been last when the horses waited at the corral gate, or drank from some pool where a spring seeped from the hills and there was only room for one horse to drink at a time. The Texas Savage, who had saved the horses in the blizzard, always stood first, nearest the gate, and drank first while the others waited, and he was extremely jealous of his rights. Let no horse crowd him, or he was met by a threatening heel, or the click of yellowed teeth.

When Pinto came home from the Fair, either because his nerves were still raw, and his temper quick, or because his new experience had made him bolder, no man can tell, he began, gradually, to work his way up the line. A rush and a snap here, a whirl of heels there, and horse after horse gave way. The process took some weeks, and with several of the older horses, the threat had to be repeated several times; but none stood to give him actual combat, and at last, he stood next in line to the gray horse at the corral gate and drank second at the narrow pools. It didn't occur to him to tackle the gray, who had been leader since Pinto could remember. For him, Pinto had a real respect.

At the extreme west end of the saddle horse pasture, where a deep and narrow arroyo heads against the hills, was a spring where the horses sometimes watered. It trickled out from the foot of a high bank, formed a shallow pool, and then lost itself in the sand. There were two ways of approach; either up the bed of the arroyo, or along a game trail which, crossing the face of the bank above the pool, came down on one side steeply. One late afternoon in October, when the crisp evening air made the thickening coats of the horses roughen against the chill, they came to water at this spring. The gray horse was drinking at the pool while the others waited respectfully, strung out in single file down the narrow draw. Pinto, however, had followed the game trail and waited above to let the gray horse take his fill, and then step down to have his turn.

A coyote, half a mile back of him in the hills, yapped his first evening call, and Pinto whirled on the narrow game trail to listen. It had been raining a little through the day, and the trail was wet. As he whirled, he slipped; the edge of the trail sloughed away, and he slithered, struggling, down the bank and lit on his side with a splash, in the pool where the gray horse drank. The Texan, surprised and angered by the splash of cold water in his face, struck like a rattle-snake, and Pinto grunted as the hard hoofs slammed his ribs. He rose with an angry surge. It was all right for the gray horse to keep the leadership, but he had no business to punish Pinto for a thing he couldn't help.

The three winters of accumulated respect vanished like an April snow in Arizona, and Pinto's head drove low to grab the gray horse's front leg; but the Savage understood and snatched his leg back in the nick of time; the pinto's teeth met with a clash on air. As his leg went back, the gray horse seized Pinto's crest and clung there shaking. It was lucky for Pinto he missed his ear. The pinto whirled away from him to break his hold and to kick him as it broke. But the old horse kept his grip, and so kept out of reach. The pinto reared as he whirled, this time towards him; and although he lifted the gray half off the ground, the hold still held, and blood was now trickling down the black-and-white neck. Pinto again drove for the gray's front leg; and the gray, hampered by his grip on the pinto, was a hair too slow. The pinto got his hold. They surged and staggered until the shallow water, in which they fought, was churned into muddy foam. It was experience, age and toughness against greenness, youth and weight. The old horse, bent only on keeping his feet, wasted no ounce of strength, but let the maddened youngster push and haul him about as he pleased; for he knew that, sooner or later, if he could stand up, the young horse would tire and the chance would then come to get his ear hold. They were like boxers in a clinch, too close to strike. The gray was pushed against the bank. He tripped but didn't fall, and lunged away from the treacherous footing. They were milling now in a staggering circle. The heavier pinto was gradually working the gray nearer and nearer the bank again; and the gray, realizing the danger of a fall, fought hard to keep away. But he was on three legs and each lunge of the pinto pushed him nearer. If the pinto could once push him against the slippery bank, the gray would lose his balance. If he fell, his hold on the pinto's crest would be broken, and once down, the pinto could savage him at will.

That morning the new man who had charge of the horses on

the Mussel Shell side used up his last tobacco, and everything being in good order on his part of the range, he started over, in the afternoon, to the home camp for a fresh supply.

As the fight in the narrow arroyo became more desperate, some of the nearer horses climbed the steep sides to get out of the way, and now stood watching the battle from above. The cowboy, crossing the pasture, noticed them, and rode up to see what they were looking at so intently. He got there just as the pinto, with a vicious lifting lunge, jambed the Texas horse against the bank. Down went the gray. The cowboy, to save him, like a flash untied his rope, ran out a loop, and with a quick flip roped the pinto, took a turn on his horn and whirled his horse. The pinto, too blind with rage to realize what was happening, was dragged backwards, striking and choking; while the beaten gray, after a struggle managed to stagger up, his left leg, torn and bleeding, held out in front.

For a minute or two, the "paint" horse struggled hard; but the cowboy was above him, and his pony, though much lighter than Pinto, with the rope at that angle could have choked a bull, and he gave in, his breath coming in great choking gasps, his legs shaking under him. The cowboy knew that to turn him loose again meant only a renewal of the fight, and when the pinto calmed down, he rode his pony along the edge of the draw, leading the maddened pinto along the bottom until a side trail allowed him to scramble out; and so they came to the home corral, the blood slowly clotting on the pinto's mane from the deep marks of the gray's teeth. That fight burned in Pinto's leadership of the saddle horses, as his fight with the brown colt had established his leadership of the yearlings, and it was never afterwards disputed.

SHOT UNDER THE WIRE A HALF LENGTH TO THE GOOD (PAGE 53)

CHAPTER X

The next winter passed in idleness for Pinto, and he grew and developed into the four-year-old that Patch had dreamed of. By the time his owner had returned from England in the spring, a plan had matured in Hinton's mind of taking the colt abroad with him the next year. Then Pinto began work in earnest, and he was schooled and bitted until he could jump four feet from a stand, or fly five in his stride; and Clark cut pine boughs and set them up to look like hedges. But Pinto didn't forget wire, and Clark would sometimes, when at exercise, or if strangers were present, ride in and out over the pasture fence.

And now came Pinto's great adventure. When the horses left for England in the autumn, he went with them, and Clark went too; for the Bull Mountain herd had grown, and now there were more horses to go abroad than Hinton could handle alone. How they crowded and snorted in the loading pens at Glendive! But it was nothing to the crowding and snorting that went on for the first day in the stock cars while the train rumbled through the North Dakota Bad Lands, and they looked out dizzily through the slats and shrank together in terror as the ground rushed underneath. The first time that the engine whistled, there was a surge to the end of the cars that would have crushed the end-horses, if they had not been loaded so tightly. At the first feeding station where they were unloaded, they neither ate nor drank; but although they lost some weight before they reached New York, and they were still homesick, the first flush of nervousness was gone.

The ship was worse. They were loaded between decks, where

they couldn't see out, and the motion of the ship kept them balancing until their muscles ached, while they felt all the pangs of seasickness without the so-called "relief" of being sick; for a horse's stomach is so constructed that he cannot throw up. At last it was over, and after a short and smooth journey in a new sort of train, Pinto found himself in a large box-stall at Melton, in a finer stable than he had ever seen. But fine though it was, the Montana horse shivered in it from the dampness of an English December, more than ever he had when exposed to the dry and bitter cold of the high plains. And then came shoes, which the range horse had never worn; and while some of them fought hard the pinto, with Clark talking to him in front and Hinton holding his foot, took it easily, for a white-man had never hurt him and Pinto thought no white-man ever would. After a week of walking exercise, Pinto began to school, but Patch was in no hurry to start him hunting. He was not for sale, and Patch wanted to wait until he was thoroughly familiar with the country and until Lord Ernest should come back from Egypt to ride him. Sometimes Clark rode him to the meet to see the hounds, but Patch was adamant about his going to a run too soon. He was the only "paint" horse at Melton, among the hundreds of English and Irish hunters—the cream of the stables of the best hunting country in the world.

And while the English pretended to scoff at his color and call him a "circus horse" (there was nothing said out loud after one smart stud-groom had laughed at him before Patch, in the bar of the "Bell"), there was many an eye of envy cast on him as he passed at exercise or came to the meets.

In February Lord Ernest came, and by that time Pinto was as fit as a prize-fighter; for the strong English oats had grown him, so that, fit as he was, he weighed a hundred pounds more than when he left the range. Lord Ernest rode him one school, and then Clark took him to a Belvoir meet. He was to be ridden second horse, so that he might be sobered a trifle by a morning's job about the country. The Belvoir had a dull morning and holed a fox after a short run at 12:18; and the big field pulled up to change horses, to eat a little, to drink a little, to smoke a little, and to talk a lot. Clark was holding Pinto and Lord Ernest's first horse, a black gelding from Palmadime. Pinto was on the left and as Clark tightened his girth, he stepped over a little bumping the black horse lightly, and the black horse, irritable from a dull morning and no gallop, slashed at him with his teeth and cut the pinto's cheek and cracked his heavy bit against the pinto's jaw. In a flash, the range horse, not wasting time to bite, with his mouth full of bits, took half a step away, and then sent both hind feet crashing into the black's flank just in front of the stifle. He hadn't forgotten the lessons of the range, and the hand-raised black horse would have caught those shod heels again if Clark had not spun the pinto towards him, head on. Lord Ernest, having finished his lunch, got up, and the Belvoir field moved off to draw, the pinto's temper still high, and Lord Ernest none too pleased to have had his black horse kicked. Pinto soon found himself in a narrow lane, wedged tightly between other horses; the jam extending as far as he could see in front and behind, while hounds were drawing a nearby gorse. Pinto didn't understand it; and then as he was staring about in wonder, he saw what Lord Ernest did not see—a fox steal from the covert, hesitate at the sight of the crowd, and slip back again. The range horse, with a squeal, started pushing his way through the other horses to the side of the lane.

Lord Ernest, annoyed, took sharp hold of his head, but the reigns were nearly jerked out of his Lordship's hands by a vicious snatch; the pinto reared, and a tall hat fell and was trampled, as the swearing British shoved out of the way. There was a low

THEY WERE MILLING NOW IN A STAGGERING CIRCLE (PAGE 58)

gate into the field. Before Lord Ernest had gathered his reins, the pinto was over it; and as tattered fragments of "damned Americans" and "circus horse" floated after him on the heavy English air, Lord Ernest, himself, mentioned a name that is not associated with the hunting field. The pinto stopped when he got to the covert, not knowing which way to go. As he hesitated, staring, the fox, pressed now by the hounds, went away on the far side; and Lord Ernest, realizing that escape from the crowd gave him a favored place, hustled Pinto down the field and around the end of the covert, just as the hounds and huntsmen came streaming out. A moment's wait to let the hounds settle on the line, and they were off. The pinto was galloping half-heartedly, for he wanted to go back and look for the fox where he had last seen him, until sinking a low bottom he caught the fox's scent, and it came to him like a light that those black-and-white dogs must be after the coyote too. Then Lord Ernest began to realize that he was riding a wonder, for he was sailing along at the top of the first flight; the "paint" horse galloping and jumping with a careful freedom that Lord Ernest did not know. They passed through a piece of woodland and into the Belvoir Vale. The range horse threaded the trees like a butterfly and floated down a stony hill where the British pulled up to walk. They crossed the close-fenced Vale and there was only a handful of the big field left—the master on a chestnut, the huntsman on a gray, a lady in a blue habit on a black American mare, three pink coats and two blacks.

Thirty throbbing minutes had passed into the rooms of memory when they came to the Park, jumped the Park wall and came down to the Wiesendine, flushed with the spring rains, just as the dripping tail hounds were clambering out on the far side. And Lord Ernest wondered, for well as he had been carried, the pinto had never before faced water. But his ears were up, and although he shortened his stroke as they splashed through the marshy ground, he again caught the scent in the lowland and went on and over with a yard to spare, while a splash to the right and left marked the toll that the stream had taken. There was a long slope out of the low country. Up this hounds were now racing. Lord Ernest, though he knew that he had never been carried so well and that he was in a run that would make Belvoir history, was horseman enough to realize that the pinto was still young and unseasoned. So he decided to pull up and follow the rest of the run as best he could at a slower pace through gates. But he failed to realize that the "paint" horse was running to kill; and when he took hold of him half-way up the slope, he was met again by a *tearing* lunge, and after a second and third pull, he found that he might just as well try to hold the Liverpool Express with his handkerchief. At the top of the rise, he was a field ahead of the nearest horseman and almost with the hounds.

A half mile further on when the pack went into a thick woodland covert, the "paint" horse wasn't twenty yards behind. Again Lord Ernest tried to stop him, and he came as near praying as he had since a boy. The "paint" horse crashed through the straggling boundary fence and went on and into the scrub, as the wild cattle on El Capitan bore through the tangled brush. Lord Ernest could only crouch along his neck. He gave up trying to guide the horse, utterly unconscious now of the man on his back, and only concerned to kill. Hat gone, the blood from his scratched face staining his white stock, Lord Ernest was gasping as they came out on the far side. There was a high and thick bullfinch between the covert's end and the next field. While the hounds checked for a moment looking for a hole, the pinto, winding the fast sinking fox, slammed through them and jumped, looking to right and left as his head came through the thorn. There, sure enough, to the left and not twenty yards away, the beaten fox was crawling up a furrow. The "paint" horse turned in the air and was on him like a hawk, and then, Lord Ernest understood. There and then, the annals of fox-hunting would have had a new chapter written, but the fox, as the pinto struck, dragged himself into a field drain, while the horse snorted and pawed, in a tiger's frenzy, at the narrow mouth. Lord Ernest was off him like a shot, and with difficulty, dragged him to one side, as the huntsman who had cut across lots came up.

Lord Ernest said nothing of what had happened; it wouldn't have been believed; and later that afternoon the pinto, now thoroughly tired, and with Lord Ernest on foot, came back to Melton. Until years later, he never told anyone but Patch and Clark what had occurred, but at Palmadime you can still see a brush with a silver tag and the legend—"Pinto"—Belvoir—Feb. 11, 1894"—and the Paint Horse Day is still famous in the Belvoir Vale.

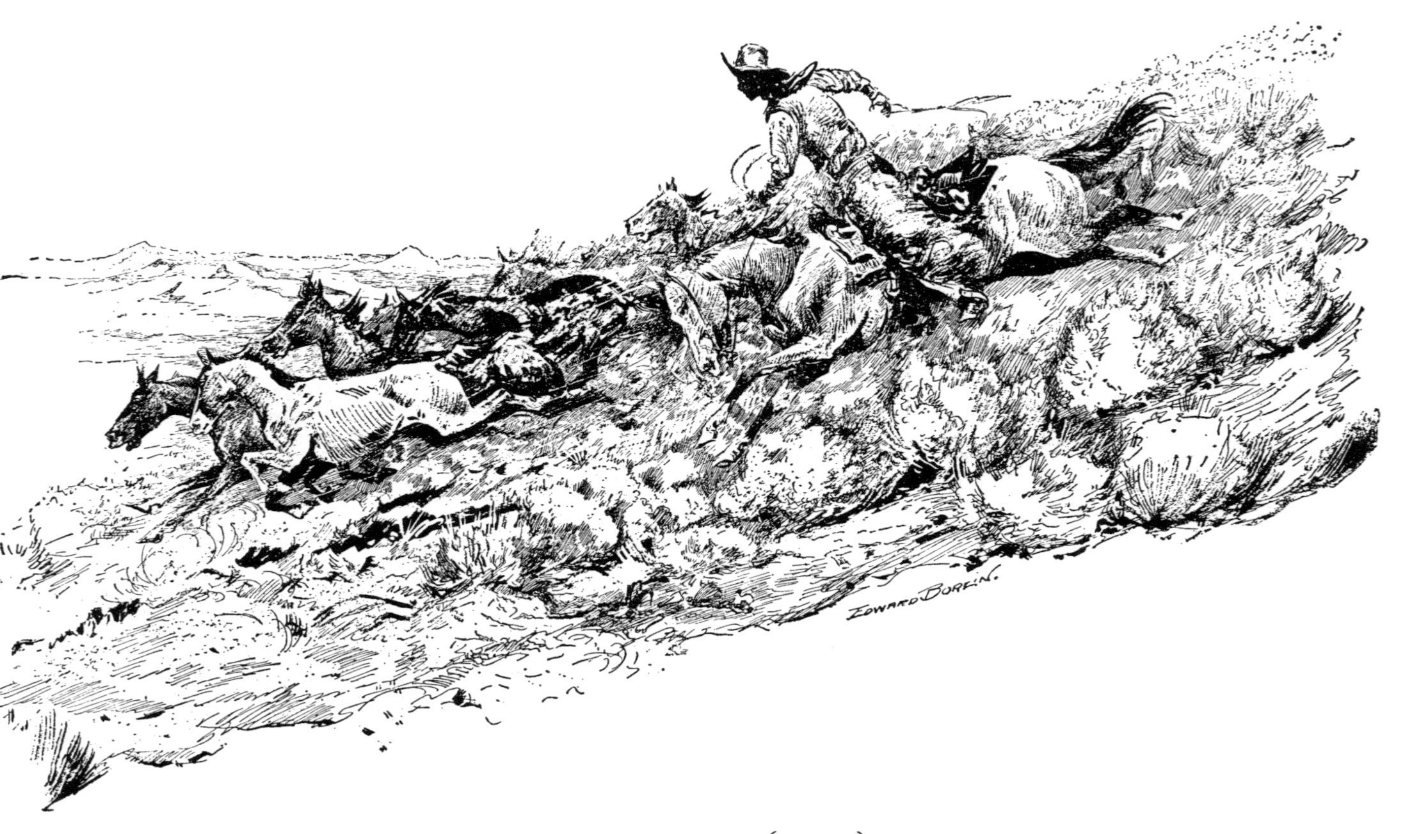

FRESH HORSES WERE ROPED (PAGE 71)

CHAPTER XI

The morning after the Belvoir Run, when Clark went to the stable, he found Pinto drooping in a corner of his stall, a fever raging—pneumonia, the Vet said—and for five days Pinto hung on the edge of death. Either Patch or Clark stayed with him day and night, fearing the worst; and then the great lungs, developed in the clear rarefied air of the Montana foothills, won; the fever's hold was broken; and Pinto, though only a shadow of himself, began to mend. By the middle of March he was well enough to travel, and started for home with Clark and Hinton. Half the stud-grooms in Melton came down to the station to see them off; even the old Earl of Palmadime, a famous thruster in his day, came also, and got out of his brougham to see the pinto loaded. They had a smooth voyage, but it was not until Pinto was unloaded at the end of the railroad journey and breathed again the air of his native hills that the brightness came back to his eye and the spring to his step.

That summer he did no work; and by the time autumn came, he was himself again, but Patch, fearing that exposure to the storms of a northern winter might be too hard on the horse after his sickness and the stabling in England, had a log barn built, and in this Pinto spent the nights when October came with its glittering, frosty evenings.

It was daybreak on the last morning of the month, and Hinton was ready to start next day for England with that season's crop of hunters, when, opening the door of Pinto's stable, he found the "paint" horse gone, and in his place, a hollow-eyed roan gelding, his gaunt flanks spur-marked and covered with a drying cake of sweat and dust.

There had been much talk of horse and cattle thieves in Montana and Wyoming for some time, but the Johnson County War had been fought in Wyoming two years before, and it was generally understood that since the organization of the Vigilantes in Montana the thieves had quit the country, some voluntarily, some by the persuasion of Judge Lynch. Their leader, however, had never been definitely accounted for. One man claimed to have seen him on an eastbound train in Dakota; some others, coming through with a trail herd from the South, were sure they had seen him playing Monte in a saloon at Dodge City. At any rate, no one had seen him in Montana for some months, and it was supposed that, finding things too hot, he had escaped to Canada. But Patch knew that the brand on the hard-ridden roan horse belonged to an outfit fifty miles north, and there couldn't be any doubt that a man, who would silently leave one horse and take another, was a fugitive. He had not long to wait, for before he had finished examining the roan, the sheriff of the next county, north, rode up with eight men, gaunt and travel-stained, their beaten horses scarcely able to trot. They wanted food and fresh horses, and while Aubrey drove in the Bull Mountain saddle horses, and the men bolted a hurried breakfast, the sheriff told his story. Early the morning before, a lone bandit had held up the Lewistown stage, killed the express messenger, and then been driven off, empty handed. He had headed south and the sheriff, advised at once, had gathered a posse and started after him, only a few hours behind. Last evening the bandit had way-laid a cowboy and taken his horse not far from the ranch where the sheriff and his posse had also changed horses.

Now, when he heard what had happened at Big Coulee, the Sheriff made his plans, for he felt sure, from the thief's boldness and from his intimate knowledge of the country, that he must be the ex-leader of the Rustlers, and in that case, felt certain that the robber would make for the rough country that borders Yellowstone Park. Fresh horses were roped for the posse, and the cavalcade, re-enforced by Hinton on the Texas Savage, started South. That afternoon, they stopped to rest their horses where Laural Creek flows into the Yellowstone, and that night they cut across a corner of the Big Horn Basin and arrived next morning, to rest again, near the sulphur springs on the Stinking Water, which gave the river its name. Old Frenchy DeMaris, who had a cabin at the Springs, told them that as he was looking for his milk cow at daybreak, he had met a silent rider on a pinto horse, hurrying towards the hills. They were only a few hours behind, but their horses must be rested, and they stayed at the Springs until afternoon, for DeMaris had only an aged pair of wagon horses, and once in the mountains they would find no more ranches with fresh mounts. Before daylight next morning, they camped on the North Fork, and cooked a meager meal in a depression screened by rocks and trees, where their fire would not show. The others fell asleep almost before the meal was finished, but Hinton, before he lay down, walked out into the little meadow where he had picketed the gray, and far up the stream saw, for a moment, the flicker of a fire, pinpricked through the blackness, and faint on the night breeze his ear caught the whinny of a distant horse. He waked the sheriff, and together they went up the trail on foot. It was black as a pocket, and once away from the feeding horses, not a sound broke the stillness. The fire had disappeared; the pinto's call had warned the bandit that other horses were near. He had doused his fire and fled.

They returned to the others, but Patch could not sleep; and the next morning, though the Sheriff protested that neither men nor horses had rested enough, they went on. They came out on the shore of Yellowstone Lake, and the hoof-prints of a single hurrying horse were plain in the dusty trail. At noon, where the trail turned up a narrow valley, the sheriff called a halt; the horses were nearly done. Patch realized that now the robber knew he was followed, he would push the pinto hard. There was not a horse in Montana that could run him down; there was no longer a chance for surprise, and Patch, deciding to play a lone hand, went on. The wild valley gradually narrowed to a gorge. By four in the afternoon, the boulder-strewn bottom was in shadow, though the sun still shone high on the towering sides. The way was rough; and the gray, tough though he was, swayed with fatigue, when suddenly Patch heard the rattle of falling stones high on his right, and looking up caught a glint of black and white, as it flashed for a second in the sunlight and vanished in the thick and stunted bull-pines that clung to the sides of the gorge. Fifty yards beyond where the pinto vanished, a baby avalanche had swept a narrow gap in the timber. Across this opening Patch knew the trail must pass, and he spurred his tired horse to be opposite it in time. The game, gray Texan struggled to respond, staggered, tripped on a boulder and fell with a groan, as a broken fore-leg crumpled under him. As the horse fell, Patch jumped clear, dragged his Winchester from the scabbard and had run forward twenty yards, when the pinto and his rider came out in the opening, far up near the canyon's lip, and Patch knew his last chance had come. He fired, and a spurt of dust sprang from the cliff, a foot from the robber's shoulder. He shot again, and the black sombrero turned half around on the bandit's head, as horse and rider disappeared in the trees.

A new life for Pinto began the night the robber stole him. Instead of firm kindness that his human friends had always shown him, he received from his new master a brutal roughness that he had never known. The first few times he was jerked and spurred, he was too much amazed to resent it, but under the rough treatment his nature began to change, and a hatred grew in him for the man he carried. Three times he tried to buck his rider off, and although he used every trick learned from the Texas Savage, and more besides that his wild nature taught him, he might as well have tried to buck off his own mane; and when he reached back to seize the robber's foot and drag him from the saddle, his teeth met instead the heavy tapaderos; and a blow across the eyes from the butt of a loaded quirt, left him stunned and half blinded.

For the first ten days the pinto horse averaged seventy miles a day; any other horse would have cracked under the strain. Southward they went, and ever southward, and the superb physique inherited from his thoroughbred English mother, combined with the wiry toughness of his wild father, stood between him and death. As the weary days passed, the docile side of his nature, acquired through generations obedient to man, was sinking into the background, and more and more the savage and untamed strain in him grew. They followed lonely trails, and met no one; but although the pinto tried open rebellion no more, he bided his time, with the instinctive and savage cunning of a wild animal. His wild rider understood the savageness of the horse he rode, and although he roughed him mounted, he never gave an opening on foot. The pinto's chafed and bleeding ankles showed how tightly he was hobbled, so that he was barely able to crop enough grass to sustain him when they stopped to make their lonely camps.

They traveled mostly at night, to avoid notice and to escape the heat, which increased as they moved south, until one broiling noon, far down in Arizona, they came to a blistered town of deserted shacks—the ruins of a golden dream. The baleful glint of scattered cans lay dead in a shroud of rust. Nothing stirred in the single, sun-baked street. The only building with the windows

THEY WILL TELL YOU THE LEGEND OF "THE PAINTED MOONBEAM" (PAGE 76)

still in was the saloon; and there the robber stopped, tied Pinto to the rail in front, kicked aside a faded dog dozing in the doorway and entered.

An hour later, when he came out, Pinto noticed he swayed a little, and that when he mounted, his legs seemed to have lost some of their panther-like spring. They left the tattered hamlet, and that afternoon, as they jogged through the blinding glare, the robber drank often from a bottle, and as he drank, his wicked roughness grew. He jerked and spurred his tired horse without mercy, and the pinto's temper, edged by weeks of abuse and hard riding, burned into him a hatred such as only the helpless and tortured victims of man may know. As the sun sank, a blazing ball among the tumbled buttes, and the violet shadows softened the western hills, they came to a lonely spring at the edge of some stunted trees. The robber swayed to the ground, too careless now to think, and dragged off his saddle and bridle; and Pinto could have jerked out of his hand the light hair neck-rope that was all that stood between him and freedom; but he stood rigid, his twitching ears the only sign of the storm within. The thief staggered to his saddle and untied the hobbles, and then as he stooped to put them on, the pinto struck, and struck again. Five minutes later, before the dust had settled on the battered, lifeless body, the pinto was flying westward, half terrified by what he had done—he had killed a human being, and, willingly, no human hand should ever touch him again. The wild side of his nature had conquered, and the man-made world that he had known was a fast fading memory.

Late that evening, topping a rise in the moonlight, he came full on a band of wild mustangs, which scattered terrified, as the great black and white horse burst upon them; but Pinto's call stopped them, and after a few wide galloping circles, they gathered around him snorting, a shy band of admirers.

He was seldom seen again. Sometimes a lone cowboy might glimpse him as he vanished around the shoulder of a sandstone butte, or see him on a sky-line as he stood for a moment cut like a cameo against the blue Arizona sky. Sometimes the riders of a far-flung rodeo came on a band of wild horses, and sometimes they had the luck to rope a pinto colt. If so, they prized him, for as time went on, the "paint" horses from that part of Arizona were thought the best horses in the Southwest. And a tale grew up among the scattered Indians, merged in their myths of the Superstition Mountains, of a great black and white horse, an offspring of the horses that draw the chariot of the Moon, which the Great Spirit had sent to Earth to regenerate their stunted ponies. Ask the Piutes, and they will tell you the legend of "The Painted Moonbeam."

The Phantom Bull

EL FANTASMO AND HIS MOTHER

THE PHANTOM BULL

∴

CHAPTER I

On a late afternoon in August in the summer of '88, Old Man Ennis rode down the Jack Creek Trail and across the meadows toward the grove of cottonwoods which marked his ranch. He was not really an old man; you could tell that by the set of his shoulders and by the erect spare figure which swayed a little to the quick-stepping Spanish walk of his buckskin horse. But as Old Man Ennis he was known and thought of for fifty miles up and down the Madison, for he had come to Montana when it was a new country, and he was old in the sense that he had helped to make its annals. Born in eastern Texas fifty years before, he had worked his way north up the Mississippi, had had a taste of border warfare on the fringe of the Civil War, and had finally been carried to Montana on the wave of adventure that swept so many bold spirits to the gold strike at Alder Gulch. After a couple of seasons as a freighter between Silver City and the new camp, he married the daughter of a Missouri emigrant, who, like himself, had been lured to Montana by the talisman of gold. Ennis and his father-in-law were stockmen by taste and by training, and they soon moved to the Upper Madison and took up the homesteads which now formed the nucleus of Old Man Ennis's large holdings.

Here they prospered, for the man from Missouri had been bred in a farming country. He realized the value of winter feed, and years before the other stockmen of Montana thought of putting up hay, the Ennis

Flats along the Madison were irrigated, and in the hard winters when his neighbors' cattle died by hundreds, Old Man Ennis's cattle came through, and his calf crop averaged seventy per cent where often his neighbors' did not average twenty per cent. And always he bought more ranches from his neighbors who came and failed, and always his ageing father-in-law preached more irrigation and more hay, until, on the August evening that I speak of, there were one thousand acres under ditch, and the Ennis cattle, with the Swinging H (H H) on their near side middle, dotted the slopes along the Madison. On their summer range you could find them in little bands as far east as the breaks of the Gallatin, and in the parks among the timber to the foot of the Spanish Peaks.

So Old Man Ennis jogged across the meadows, his hand-wrought spurs tinkling gently and the sunlight glinting on the silver inlay of his Spanish bit and on the conchas of hammered silver that covered the cheek-pieces of his ear bridle. For Old Man Ennis was a Personage, in his way a swell; and, unlike the Montana cowboys, he used the rig of a California vaquero.

Those were the days before the professional Rodeos and Roundups and Frontier Days, with their hired exhibitions of the cowboy's art. There were few fences and fewer corrals; cattle were worked and horses broken in the open; and while the Montana cowboys frankly said they did not savvy the Old Man's deeply carved, single-cinch California saddle, with its stirrups hung a little forward and covered by heavy tapaderas, they as frankly admitted that when it came down to the business of the range, there wasn't a cowboy in Montana that could take the shine off the

Old Man. And certainly it would have puzzled a modern rodeo professional, with his hunched-up seat and his bucking rolls, to have ridden one of Old Man Ennis's 'Comet' colts across the open benches without pulling leather.

Old Man Ennis had begun to realize that his cattle if better bred would bring higher prices, and in this he was encouraged by his son Walter who was taking a course at an Eastern agricultural college. Accordingly, during the next Christmas vacation they met in Chicago, went East together, and at Marietta, Ohio, they bought an eighteen-months-old Hereford bull, Primrose Chieftain XII, and three imported heifers. In the spring, Walter brought Chieftain and the heifers to Montana. When the freight car in which they were loaded was shunted to the stock-pens at Manhattan, Old Man Ennis was on hand to help unload them. During the next three days, as they traveled slowly up the Madison Valley toward the home ranch, half the men in Madison County came to have a look at the Old Man's 'full bloods'; for these were the first pure-bred Herefords to be brought into that part of the State, and there was much curiosity to see them and much speculation as to whether range cattle, crossed with 'fancy stock,' could survive the hard conditions of the Montana range.

Primrose Chieftain spent his first summer in one of the large fenced meadows near the home ranch, with the three heifers and the ranch milk cows, and when the cold and snow of winter hit Montana, and the bitter wind whistled across the wide valley, he lived with the others in the sheds near the hay corral. He grew and thickened and throve, while his muscles hardened and swelled under the constant exercise, until, when April came and the new grass began to show green again, he weighed as much as a show bull of his own age and at the same time he had a lustiness and activity that no stall-fed show bull ever acquired.

All through the winter, Chieftain had been able to see from the corral the other Ennis cattle being fed from the haystacks in the open valley; for Old Man Ennis never overstocked his range and never kept more cattle than he could hay-feed during the winter, and when in May the other cattle were driven into the hills to their summer range, a great curiosity grew in the young bull to follow them and to find out where they had gone. But Old Man Ennis had no idea of exposing Chieftain to the chances of a life on the open range, and realizing that the bull was likely to become restless, he warned his cowboys that on no account and on no occasion must the gates be left open from the pasture near the house where the milk cows and the pure-breds were to spend the summer, as they had the year before.

How long Chieftain might have respected the stout barbed wire of the pasture fence no one can tell, and it was never necessary to guess, for in early June a stranger, passing up the valley with a pack-horse, turned into the pasture to camp for the night and left in the morning without closing the gate. It was Old Man Ennis's daily habit to look at Chieftain and the others and to ride the pasture fence to make sure that all was as it should be; but that morning, seeing the cattle not far from the house at breakfast time and being unusually busy, he went about his day's work without discovering the open gate. Toward noon Chieftain and the cows had grazed across the meadow, and at about the time when they would otherwise have taken their midday drink and lain down to chew their cud and rest for a couple of hours in the spring sunshine, they came to the open gate. With a low bellow of satisfaction, Chieftain led through and, followed by the cows, started up the Jack Creek Trail, where he had seen the range cattle disappear a few weeks before on the way to their summer range. The heifers and the cows had little incentive for the new adventure, and stopped to graze on the new bunch grass as they slowly wandered up the narrow valley. Chieftain, however, filled with curiosity to find out what had become of the other cattle, did not stop to feed, but kept on up the trail, rumbling deep in his throat and occasionally stopping to give a half-dozen ringing calls and to listen for an answer, as is the habit of bulls when hunting new company.

By three in the afternoon, where the Jack Creek Valley narrows to a gorge from which the high open hillsides go up on either hand, he heard an answering challenge, and looking upward he saw against the skyline four small objects which he recognized as cattle. He challenged again and an answering challenge came floating down the hill. Without hesitation Chieftain turned off the trail and started angling up the steep hillside, stopping now and then to paw the loose gravelly soil and to roar out the notice of his coming

in the language of cattle. And always an answering call came back. As he got nearer, a red-and-white bull left the others and came down the hill to meet him, stopping, as Chieftain did, to paw and to bellow, until, when they were twenty yards apart, they stopped to look each other over, and each, rumbling angrily with his head close to the ground, pawed up a shower of loose dirt and broken sage. Then the range bull charged, and as they crashed together head on, Chieftain, although he kept his feet, was pushed backwards fifteen feet down the steep hillside. For a moment they stood panting, heads low and together; then the range bull stepped sideways quickly, and before Chieftain could guard himself a wide crimson slash in his shoulder showed where the other's long sharp horn had found its mark. But that sidestep lost the range bull the advantage of the hill and the two were now on equal terms; what meant even more, Chieftain's feeling of curiosity had been consumed in the wave of rage and pain which now gripped him, and the finish could end only in one of two ways. The stronger bull would break through the other's guard, and, when this happened, the weaker bull would be thrown down and gored, unless, when his guard broke, he was quick enough to make his escape before he was thrown. They pushed and struggled along the steep hillside and, although the range bull was quicker on his feet, Chieftain had the best of the weight. After a few vain efforts to repeat the side-stepping maneuver, the range bull, realizing that it was only a question of time until he should be overpowered and that he had best make his escape while he was still fresh enough to make a run for it, suddenly whirled off down the hill and in a few moments disappeared over the brow of the nearest ridge.

Chieftain watched him out of sight, panting, and then, getting his wind, turned up the hill to investigate the other cattle which had gradually drawn near the fighters. There were five of them, two yellowish-red cows with red-and-white calves, and a long-legged, slate-colored cow with upright horns, quite different from her companions. The odd-looking, slate-colored cow was part Zebu and had come from the low country along the Gulf of Mexico in southern Texas. In that part of the United States, as in many other warm countries, cattle suffer from the scourge of ticks, which not only weaken their hosts by infesting them in large numbers and draining their blood, but which, at the same time, give them the disease called 'tick' or 'Texas' fever. Years before it had been found that, for some reason, the sacred cattle of India, called Zebus or Brahmas, were immune to Texas fever, and the cattle-breeders of the Gulf counties of Texas imported Zebus in large numbers and crossed them with the native stock. The result was a long-legged, hardy, wild and active animal, likewise immune to Texas fever, and in every way suited to withstand the heat of the southern ranges.

The slate-colored cow was one of these Zebu cross-breds, and had come north some years before with a drove of Texas cows that Old Man Ennis had bought to stock his Montana range. She was the only Zebu in the lot, and certainly she was the cowboy's curse, for in the broken country where the cattle ranged, the slate-colored cow could outfoot a horse. She jumped the wire fences of the valley meadows like a ranch-raised greyhound, and taught the other cattle to hide in the quaking asp thickets along the little streams that tumble down to the Madison, as her mother had taught her to hide in the timbered breaks along the southern bayous that wander idly toward the Gulf. The cowboys would have shot her years before as a renegade and a disturber of the peace, but the willful adventuress struck a chord in Old Man Ennis's sympathetic heart. He, too, had come north from Texas and, like the slate-colored cow, had struggled and won against the odds of a new environment, and while he sometimes cursed her with his lips, as he failed to head her in a sliding rush down a broken slope, or spurred his saddle horse in vain to catch her on an open hill, there was always in his heart a glow of admiration for her when she beat him.

Old Man Ennis found Chieftain after a few days' search and drove him back to the home ranch with the two cows and their red-and-white calves. Neither the Old Man nor his cowboys, however, saw the slate-colored cow again after the day that Chieftain was found, until the next December, for she spent the summer with a band of elk high up on the headwaters of the Madison, and did not come back to the home ranch until the first heavy snows drove the elk down to the lower country.

She spent the winter quietly enough with the other Ennis cattle around the haystacks, and left again alone the following spring, three weeks before the other cattle were turned out on the summer range. She made her way deliberately and slowly to a little basin that she knew of tucked away far up near the foot of the Spanish Peaks. There, under the overhanging branches of a mountain cedar, was born to her a slate-colored bull calf, in all respects like his mother's Zebu forebears, except for a six-inch band of white which extended diagonally across his face from above the right eye, down and across the left nostril. It was as if

Nature, intending to give the calf the even white face of his Hereford father, had been hurried a little in the making and had allowed her usually accurate hand to slip sideways.

Until he was four months old, the slate-colored calf with the strange-looking white face never left the little basin where he was born, although gradually as he grew in strength he followed his mother greater distances when she grazed; but she never allowed him to go with her on her daily trip for water down the long steep hill to Mill Creek. The cow made that trip to water every day about noon, and she taught her calf that when she left he must lie perfectly flat with his head and neck stretched out along the ground, hidden in a bed of tall ferns which grew in the center of the basin. The old cow knew that the coyotes and the bears and the mountain lions which might devour the calf, if they found him alone, hunt by scent more than by sight. She knew also that a calf or a fawn lying perfectly still gave off almost no scent at all, so that if the calf kept out of sight in the tall ferns there was little chance of his being found by a wandering beast of prey.

One day in early August, when the cow had gone for water and the calf lay hidden in his bed of ferns, a two-year-old black bear ambled over the rim of the little basin intent on looking for grubs under some mouldering logs which lay among the ferns and under which he had found especially fat grubs the summer before. He came shambling down the slope, stopping to turn over the loose rocks, for the crickets which lived underneath them were good eating too, and made a pleasant aperitif for the slugs which were to come. He stopped now and then to examine with his sensitive nose the breeze which came wandering down from the Spanish Peaks, and once he gave a sort of snarling grunt as the breeze brought him the scent of a mountain lion; but he could tell that the lion was a long way off, for the wild animals read the breeze as understandingly as a person reads a newspaper. It is a newspaper which for them is being printed every minute, and which they can read in daylight or darkness, whether they are moving or still, and which carries for them a warning even when they are asleep.

As the bear came down into the basin, he smelt also the strong scent of the cow, but he paid little attention to it, for although the black bears would eat beef if they found a carcass, they were too small to kill cattle. That was left for the grizzlies, and even the grizzlies did it only in exceptional cases. The bear looked about with his small pig-like eyes to see if he could locate the cattle which he smelled so strongly; seeing nothing, he started into the bed of ferns to look for the grubs, and headed straight for the spot where the calf lay crouched along the ground.

If the bear had passed twenty feet to the right or to the left, the terrified calf, which had smelled the strange and awful smell of the moving bear, would have lain still and the bear would have passed without notice, for the still calf gave off little or no scent, and the air all about him was already tainted with the smell of the cow. But the black bear came straight on until the terrified calf could see his dark hulk through the fern stems. Then with a bawl of terror he scrambled to his feet and, with his little tail stiff with fear, went bounding through the ferns in the direction in which he had seen his mother disappear. For a moment the bear hesitated with surprise, and then started in pursuit, for there was no doubt in his mind that young veal was a far finer dinner than grubs, and here was an almost unheard-of chance of getting the veal without danger, while the grubs would be there for another day.

Now a strong four-months-old calf can run quite fast for a short distance, but a bear, clumsy and awkward as he looks, can run even faster, and, although the calf had a start of twenty feet, it would only be a few seconds before a blow from that shaggy black paw would knock him helpless. Luckily the calf ran straight, giving the bear no advantage of a turn, and luckily also this calf had inherited the activity of his Zebu ancestors. He jumped in his stride a windfall of logs which the bear had to climb over, and all the time as he ran his terrified bawling filled the little basin.

Meanwhile the slate-colored cow had taken her fill at Mill Creek, and grazing as she came back up the steep hillside, had reached the edge of the basin when the calf's first terrified call reached her. With a low roar of rage she broke from her rambling walk into a

run with a quickness that would have puzzled a quarter-horse, and as she came along to where the edge of the basin breaks away toward Mill Creek, she saw fifty yards from her the calf with the bear not two feet behind him and about to strike. She had been running fast before, but now with a bellow of fury she hurled herself into the basin with a rush to which fear and rage lent an extra wing, and the bear's paw, raised to strike, was used to stop himself instead, for that angry roar took away his appetite for veal like an illness. He turned to run for shelter in the berry bushes which grew in clusters along the floor of the valley, and had nearly reached them when he found that it was hopeless. He turned to face his pursuer, rearing and striking at the very second when the cow, her head low, hit him amidships. Down they went, the bear over backwards, the cow on her knees. The bear was gasping, for his wind was gone, and a bloody furrow along the

cow's neck showed where the bear's blow had landed. If that blow had been given by a grizzly, the cow would never have regained her feet, but as it was, the pain of the tearing blow only added fury to her second charge. Again the bear reared and struck, but this time his blow lacked force and, although it tore away more skin from the cow's neck, it checked her not at all. He was thrown and gored again and again, until, as the fight worked nearer the bushes and the cow began to tire, he managed, in a moment when she stopped to catch her breath, to drag himself into the thicket; and the cow, after much head-shaking and bellowing, went slowly to join the calf which had stood trembling behind her.

CHAPTER II

THE cow gave up hiding the calf after the day that the bear found him, and as he was now strong enough to follow his mother wherever she went, they left the basin where he was born and spent the rest of the summer in the high, park-like country at the foot of the Spanish Peaks, from which they could see, spread out like a map below them, the long and wide valleys of the Gallatin and the Madison to a point where their fringe of green merged and they joined the Jefferson at Three Forks and became the Missouri.

The slate-colored cow's instincts were more like those of a wild animal than like those of ordinary cattle, and the calf acquired the knowledge and habits of the young elk and deer that they often met, and with which the cow was on a friendly if not an intimate footing. They fed mostly at night, and after daylight took refuge in the quaking asp thickets which clothed every stream. When the flies were bad in the thickets, they lay down for the day on some high and open ridge where the strong breeze kept the flies away, and from which they could see the country for miles in every direction. When from some such lookout they occasionally saw Old Man Ennis or some of his cowboys, the old cow taught the calf not to gallop off in a straight line regardless of cover, as other cattle did, but to slip away as a wolf does, careful to take advantage of every rock and tree and piece of broken ground.

Sometimes the breeze carried them the scent of a bear, or they might see one in the chokeberry thickets, and then the cow would paw the ground and shake her long sharp horns while the calf huddled against her. She taught the calf to keep away from a place where the mountain lion scent came from; she taught him that he must not eat the sweet-smelling blue larkspur, which is death; she taught him not to remain for long in the company of other cattle, because sooner or later where there were cattle there came cowboys. She taught him to come only at night to the places where Old Man Ennis salted the cattle; and she taught him, once he had taken refuge in the timber, to lie down and stay still instead of crashing through it and making a noise which would tell anyone where he was. She taught him how always to give the porcupine and the skunk the courtesy of the trail, and she taught him to stand stock-still and watch carefully if he saw the grouse flush suddenly, until he knew what had disturbed them. She taught him of a steep hidden trail, known only to the deer, by which they could cross the Jack Creek Canyon and so get from the Gallatin to the Madison without having to go twelve miles around the canyon head.

She introduced the calf to her friends the elk that lived near the head of the Gallatin, for from them he could learn the best mountain pastures, as well as how to get through the steep high country where a horse could not follow. She introduced him to the band of antelope that lived on the Madison benches, from whom he could learn where the best feed was in the lower country.

She showed him the great black stallion that was king of the wild horses on the Flats of the Madison, the bane of the Madison Valley ranchers, whose mares he stole; and she taught him that if there was crust on the snow in winter, a little feed could be gleaned by following the horses that pawed through the crust as cattle had never learned to do. She taught him always to avoid a trail that led through the rimrock, lest a mountain lion might spring upon his back before he could gather speed for escape or prepare for defense. She took him on a cautious visit to the old and solitary buffalo bull that lived on the head of Mule Creek. It was a cautious visit, because, when a bull gets old and begins to lose his vigor, some younger bull drives him from the herd, and he spends the rest of his life in morose solitude, discontented and disagreeable, ready to attack anything or anyone. And so, by the time the first snows came in September, the splash-faced calf with his budding horns had begun to lose the wide-eyed, innocent look of babyhood and had acquired a range of knowledge and experience greater than any other youngster of his kind.

As the weather became colder, the cow and calf moved into the lower country, but it was not until January that they joined the other cattle at Old Man Ennis's haystacks. The old cow could have wintered with the elk or the wild horses, but she wanted her queer-looking calf to have the benefit of regular and strong feed, and she felt very certain that Old Man Ennis would not undertake to brand him until warm weather should come in the spring. In this she was right, for, although the Old Man and the cowboys examined the splash-faced calf as carefully as they could the first morning that they found the cow and calf with the other cattle, they did not attempt to take any liberties, for the slate-colored cow, instead of making off as she usually did when a mounted man came in sight, stood her ground head-on to the horsemen, while the big calf crowded against her. The cowboys knew, by the way the old cow shook her head and occasionally pawed the frozen ground, that she would charge at the first move of aggression on their part, and then, if someone was not very quick with his gun, it would mean a gored cow-horse and very likely a gored man. So she was unmolested, a sort of privileged freebooter, for she prodded the other cattle away from the hay until she and the calf had finished and took for herself and for him the most sheltered spots in the timbered bottoms where the cattle stayed when a bad storm was raging.

When the first new blades of green grass began to show, the cow, with the calf, now a yearling, left the Madison meadows, and, taking the road up the valley late in the evening, passed the next day with some other cattle at a hay ranch twenty miles farther toward Henry's Lake; the next night, having made twenty miles more, she turned up Wall Creek to a meadow where her friends the elk were wintering.

The splash-faced calf's second summer was passed, as before, on Old Man Ennis's summer range. Often they saw the Old Man or some of his cowboys. Sometimes the Old Man saw them as they whisked into the timber or vanished off a ridge where they had lain down for the day; and there grew in the Old Man a great respect for the slate-colored cow and a determination to put his Swinging H on the big yearling bull with the queer white splash across his face.

When the first cutting of alfalfa was passed and there was a lull in the summer's work, the Old Man gathered his neighbors and all the cowboys he and they could muster, and with a remuda of saddle horses and a pack outfit with food and supplies to last a week, camped on the head of Cherry Creek, determined to ride the country until the cow and calf could be caught and the latter branded. The Old Man brought with

him also his cattle dogs, which the cattle feared and hated, for the dogs could harry them through the thickest timber where horsemen could not penetrate, and finally force them into the open, barking all the time to let the cowboys know where they were and in which direction the unseen cattle were moving. The Old Man offered the price of a new hat for the first man to put a rope on the splash-faced calf, but definite orders were given that neither the cow nor the calf should be hurt.

The first day's hunt, which covered the country eastward toward the Gallatin, showed many cattle, but not a trace of the slate-colored cow, although the Old Man with his field-glasses combed each succeeding valley and open hillside before he showed himself on the sky-line. The second morning the outfit on fresh horses was off as soon as it was light enough to see, and by seven o'clock, far along toward where the country breaks away to the Jack Creek Canyon, the Old Man through his glasses saw the cow and calf cross an open meadow and enter a wide stretch of timber that covered the mountain-side above the gulch. He marked the place where the cattle disappeared. The dogs were sent in at the point where the cattle had vanished, and it was only a few minutes before their furious barking and a crashing among the trees showed that the chase was on.

The Old Man knew that the cattle would go through the belt of timber and come out into the open country several miles beyond, or, if they turned back, they would come out not far from where they had entered. The timber was too thick to ride through. To start around it after the course of the hunt could be decided would allow the cow and calf to come out on the far side and escape long before the cowboys could get there, for the cattle could go through the timber like elk, and to go around it was fully six miles with half the distance uphill.

Without waiting, therefore, to learn which way the cow would go, he sent Walter and three men hell-for-leather around the other side to meet the cattle if they broke that way, while he with the others rode their horses into the edge of the timber where they could not be seen and where they could wait and listen until they knew in which direction the cow went.

For a moment the chase seemed to be stationary, and the Old Man took down his reata, thinking that the cow might break his way; and then amid the frantic barking of the dogs there came the frightened bellow of the yearling as a dog heeled him. The receding crashing among the trees showed that the cattle were hurrying away, until at last there was silence, touched more and more lightly by the faint barking of the dogs as a stronger eddy of the morning breeze swept along the hillside.

Meanwhile Walter and the others had reached the far side of the timber, and, hearing the chase coming in their direction, backed their horses into the edge of the pines and, tense with excitement, waited for the cattle to break cover. Nearer and nearer came the smash and crash of timber and the mad barking of the dogs, until within a hundred yards it stopped for a moment and then turned back upon itself, growing gradually fainter, until, when nearly out of hearing, it stopped entirely. The slate-colored cow had caught the horsemen's scent in time, and, certain now that it was no mere chance that brought the dogs after her, she sought the hidden game trail into the canyon that her friends the deer had shown her.

Old Man Ennis made his way slowly around the timber. He knew that he could not get to the other side in time to help, and he felt sure that he would find the cow and calf captive, or at least hear a story of adventurous failure, for Walter was nearly as good a hand with a rope as the Old Man himself, and the two men that were with him would have made the best modern rodeo roper look like a schoolboy with a clothesline. When he heard Walter's story, he let loose a string of profanity as rare as it was ornate, and then, as his puzzled eye rested for a moment on the wide bare hillside, which sailed up from the far side of the canyon, he saw two black specks break from the fringe of green on the canyon's farther side, and his glasses told him that they were the cow and calf and that some smaller specks were the dogs.

That ended the chase for that day, for it was a day's ride around the head of the canyon. That night the footsore and tired dogs straggled into camp, and the next day the whole outfit moved out around the head of the canyon and camped on the Madison side.

Next morning they started again at daylight. The dogs were too sore and tired to go, but Walter and the other men were sent to a point ten miles south. From this point they would beat the country back toward the canyon. Old Man Ennis felt sure that, if the cow and calf could be found and pressed hotly, they would try to recross the canyon at the place where they had crossed two days before, and he took up his station in the fringe of scrub timber that extended to within fifty yards of the canyon's edge. He had not as long to wait as he had expected, for the calf had been tired after the previous chase, and the Zebu cow had stopped to let him rest where there was good grass and water at the head of a small creek scarcely two miles from the canyon. There the cow and calf were lying when just at sunup they saw Walter and the others as they rode across the creek a mile below. The cow did not move until the horsemen were out of sight. Then she jumped to her feet, gave the calf a none too gentle hint with her horns that it was time to hurry, and started off toward the canyon.

The Zebu cow knew that the men had not seen her, and, although they had been riding in the opposite direction from that in which she was now going, she understood that the presence of horsemen on that side of the canyon meant that the hunt was still on and that she had best return to the protection of the timber on the farther side. So, although the absence of the dogs made great haste unnecessary, and to remain undiscovered was now more important than to hurry, she made her way toward the canyon at a steady jog until she came to the belt of timber in which Old Man Ennis was hiding and into which she slipped like a gray shadow. The calf, warned by some subtle communication from his mother, was as careful as the old cow to avoid making a sound.

Old Man Ennis had expected that the cow, badly frightened by her experience with the dogs, would go much farther from the canyon than she had gone before she stopped to rest, and, after having hidden his horse, he had sat down with his back against a tree and had lighted a cigarette, secure in the comforting thought that if one of the riders was lucky enough to find the cow, he would have ample warning by the noise of the oncoming chase. From where he sat he could look down the Jack Creek Canyon and see framed by the contours of its last high hills a vignette of the distant valley in which a splash of deeper green showed where his home nestled under the giant cottonwoods. As he smoked in the quiet sunlight, his mind drifted backward through the years to an afternoon when the cottonwoods were saplings; to an afternoon when he had reached home to find his dooryard crowded with hostile Indians and in time to see his wife rush from the cabin and, undaunted by numbers, snatch her screaming baby from a threatening savage. Now, by a hazy sequence of thought there took shape in his mind a realization that his wife's unquestioning instinct to save her son had a parallel in the Zebu cow.

Old Man Ennis had hidden himself exactly opposite the point where the deer trail went into the canyon. The ground between was open and sloped sharply for nearly fifty yards to the few bull-pines that grew along the edge, and it was the Old Man's plan to rope the calf as he covered this open ground.

The Zebu cow, meanwhile, was making her careful way through the timber straight toward the hidden enemy; the faint breeze blew from her toward the unseen man and horse, and the thick green timber hid them from sight. When she had come to within twenty yards, the Old Man's horse caught her scent and moved nervously; a shifting eddy of the breeze bringing to her sensitive nostrils the smell of tobacco, she knew instantly that Man lurked in front of her, and, determined to gain the shelter of the canyon at any cost, she charged. Old Man Ennis had jumped to his feet at the first sign of the horse's alarm and instinctively drew his forty-five and shot from his hip as he saw the cow's head not twenty feet away. The bullet struck a horn glancing. The shock turned the cow slightly and, with a mingled roar of rage and pain, she passed by the Old Man and his snorting horse. Plunging down the steep hillside with the terrified calf scrambling in her wake, she disappeared over the edge of the canyon, thirty yards ahead of the Old Man, who scarcely knew whether he was disgusted at his failure or relieved at her escape.

These last two adventures that the Zebu cow had had with Old Man Ennis convinced her that she and the calf were no longer safe on her old range. She crossed the canyon, laid up for a night and a day in the heavy timber on the other side, and then for the next four nights traveled steadily until she found her friends the elk high up on the head of Indian Creek near the top of the Continental Divide above Henry's Lake. The next winter she and her calf, who was now nearly two years old, spent with the elk in a sheltered basin not far from where Indian Creek flows into the Madison, where the grass was plentiful, where timber along the stream made a convenient hiding-place in case of danger and a shelter from heavy storms, and where some warm springs provided water that did not freeze even in the coldest weather.

That was a happy season for the slate-colored pair, for the Zebu cow felt that the calf was rapidly attaining an age where he could look after himself, and the young bull in his growing strength bossed the elk to his heart's content. Then, one April morning, just as the cattle and their friends the elk were getting ready to leave the sheltered basin and to follow the disappearing snow back into the hills, a shot rang out and then two more. At the first shot the young bull saw his mother crumple to her knees; at the second and third shots he felt a red-hot streak along his ribs and saw the Zebu cow tumble over on her side with a gurgling bellow. The terrified elk with the young bull in their midst fled crashing up the mountain.

That night the bald-faced bull came back to look for his mother. He slipped down through the timber without a sound, and, made frantic by the smell of blood and by grief at his mother's loss, charged her two murderers who lay rolled in their blankets near a dying fire. The roar of the maddened bull and the yells of his helpless victims rang through the sheltered basin, until all that remained were two shapeless, silent bundles, which lay in the wreckage of what once had been a camp. Far out on the Madison Flats a pair of gray wolves stopped hunting jack-rabbits to listen, and their hackles lifted as they licked their chops and trotted stealthily to see what it all meant. Finally there was silence except for the rumbling of an angry bull which grew fainter as he climbed the mountain.

CHAPTER III

THE horror of his mother's death and the memory of the nightmare rage which filled him when he gored and trampled her murderers drove the young bull headlong through the hills. For two days and two nights, stopping only to drink as he crossed the mountain streams, he fled northward until he found himself in a wild and broken country which is now the Glacier National Park.

He was in a country only penetrated by an occasional lone prospector. The deer and elk and mountain sheep remained undisturbed, for at that time hunters could still find game in the lower country. The bull spent his two-year-old summer in the high mountains above timber-line, and even when the first autumn snows came and the elk and mountain sheep moved into the lower valleys, he stayed on until, in the late fall, when the snow lay deep on the high open pastures, he too was forced by hunger to seek lower levels. Passing down the mountains he came to a snug basin, where the great winter storms which swept down from the north were broken by the surrounding hills, and he could find both food and shelter in the quaking asp and willow thickets which fringed the basin on all sides.

On one side of the basin he discovered a ledge overhung with stunted pines, under which he found some protection in the bitter winter nights, and managed to eke out a bare living by browsing on the dry leaves and smaller branches of the brush. Strong though he was, and fit as he had been when he left the high country in the autumn, March found him only a shadow of himself. Fortunately spring came early, and there were none of the late storms which so often sweep through Montana and reap a toll of death among cattle and wild game weakened by the scant feed and exposure of the long northern winter.

One sunny morning in middle April, a grizzly, that had slept away the winter in a cavernous hole made by the uprooting of a giant pine that had blown over the previous summer, roused himself from his long sleep and came shambling down the mountain through the soft snow. He was gaunt and tattered, his coat was rusty and his temper was rough. He was hungry, and his mouth slobbered as the breeze brought him the bull's scent, and he mended his pace a little. Ordinarily he was content to live on grubs, berries, and carrion when he could find it, but he was not above killing his own meat when the chance offered, and his long fast now gave him a double incentive.

The breeze was in the bear's favor and the bull never realized that an enemy was near until, as he pushed his way through a willow thicket, he came face to face with the grizzly not ten feet off. The bull had never forgotten or forgiven bears, remembering the terror of the day when as a small calf the black bear nearly had him for luncheon. Without hesitating, he dropped his head and charged. A black bear might have tried to avoid the headlong attack, but this was a grizzly of the high ranges, the king of the mountains for twenty miles, and with a snarling grunt the bear rose on his haunches, and, taking a half-step sideways, brought his great paw down with a crash on the bull's neck. It was lucky for the bull that weakened by his long fast the great bear was only half himself, for, as it was, the bull, though he did not fall, plowed forward in the snow on his knees and head, and blood spurted high from the deep red furrows in his neck where the grizzly's heavy claws had struck. With a half-smothered bellow he slid to a stop and whirled and charged again. Most bulls would have charged blindly and straight, not profiting by the dearly bought lesson, but the splash-faced bull's Zebu ancestors had maintained themselves against claw and fang and horn, and it had bred in them a wary and vicious cunning which came now to their descendant's aid; for as the bear rose to step sideways and repeat the blow, the bull with a wicked swing of his head caught his enemy fairly below his ribs and a long sharp horn pierced deep into his side. With a roar of pain the bear swept his great forearms around the bull's neck, while at the same time with his hind feet he raked the bull's breast and forelegs. Sorely as the bull was punished, the bear reached no vital spot, while the bull, with his sharp horns buried in the bear's body was literally tearing his adversary to pieces. It could not last long, and the bear with a final spasmodic struggle sank back with a gasp, dragging the bull down with him.

For a full ten minutes the bull, streaming with blood,

lay across his dead enemy, too exhausted to disengage his horns from the bear's body. At last he struggled to his knees and, throwing the bear to one side with a final effort, staggered off to his shelter under the pine-protected rock. Here he stayed until the next morning, and then, though stiff and sore from his wounds, he managed to make his way to the edge of the meadow where the melting snow had exposed a patch of last season's grass.

By the middle of June the bull was himself again, and now at three years old he was a monster among bulls. The heaviest Short Horn would have outweighed him a little, but he was a hand taller than any Short Horn, and his great frame was built, not only for strength, but for a speed and activity with which no Short Horn or Hereford could compare.

As the season advanced, the bull became more and more restless, and a hunger grew in him to mingle again with his own kind. He ranged the mountains far and wide, and even an old male cougar, which for years had given way to no mountain animal, not even the grizzly, slunk snarling aside only to be chased up a stunted pine by the bull which became more morose as he became more lonely. Each evening he stood at sunset on some hilltop and called and called in vain. By the end of July the sullen bull would charge anything that came near him, even his old friends the elk, and then on a clear moonlight night some instinct gripped him. Forgotten was the fear of men, forgotten the horror of his mother's death. With a low, rumbling bellow he started south in a long swinging trot and never stopped except to drink, until two days later he climbed the east slopes of the Madison and came to Old Man Ennis's range where he was born.

Here there were many cattle, but the splash-faced bull was not of the kind that stays long with any particular bunch, and, although he hid in the timber by day, by night he roamed the range. It was not many weeks before Old Man Ennis and his cowboys were riding their ponies sore-footed to locate the strange bull which the Old Man knew must have come to his range, for his pure-bred Hereford bulls were leaving the other cattle and coming down to the home ranch, some of them torn and bleeding from wounds which the old cowman knew could only be made by sharp horns. One of them he never found, and the coyotes could have told him that what they and the bears had left of the lost bull lay in a little meadow at the head of Mill Creek, where in the pride of his strength he had made the fatal mistake of disputing the lordship of the range with the splash-faced newcomer.

By the end of August, the latter began to enlarge the scope of his nightly journeys and to go down into the valleys of the Madison and the Gallatin to visit among the farmers' milk cows and feed in the alfalfa fields. He could jump the wire fences like a stag; there wasn't a wooden gate in the country that he couldn't knock into kindling with a heave of his great head, and though he never went into the same neighborhood two nights running, he did all the damage he could when he arrived in the fenced country. Sometimes for several nights he would remain in the hills, and then some night on the lower Madison a farmer would be awakened by the barking of his dog, and next morning he would find his fences down, his gates broken, and his horses and cattle scattered all over the valley. The next night perhaps the same thing would happen on the Gallatin, twenty miles away. The great bull left his tracks in the dust of the roads and in the mud along the irrigating ditches, but the most that was ever seen of the marauder was a gray shadow that faded into the darkness.

The farmers began to talk of a Phantom Bull, and Sam Stevenson, riding home late at night from a dance on Pole Creek, came face to face with a bald-faced shadow at a turn in the road, and afterwards swore that, although the thing charged him with the bellow of a bull, no living bull could run his roan quarter-horse at such a pace up the valley. He said that the thing, whatever it was, paid no attention to bullets, although he emptied his forty-five so near that he could not miss. The final outrage came when the Ennis storekeeper, driving his best girl home in the evening, had his new sidebar buggy smashed to kindling and his team run off; and that was not the worst of it, the young lady had her arm broken and the storekeeper was in bed for a week with a sprained back.

The last outrage was too much, and the next Saturday evening at a meeting held at the Ennis store, it was agreed that an organized hunt should be made to rid the country of a creature that had grown from a nuisance to a menace. By common consent, Old Man Ennis was elected the leader. Knowing well that the only way to deal with the situation was first to locate the quarry, he selected the six men best acquainted with the surrounding country, divided them into parties of two, and, giving each pair a pack-horse and a week's provisions, he started them out with orders to comb the country and send one man back to report as soon as the game had been found. Three evenings later, one of the pair that had been riding the breaks along the east side of the Madison, rode his sweating horse up to Old Man Ennis's ranch-house, and reported that he and his partner had marked down in The Pot a queer-looking animal that they thought was a bull.

The Pot was a cuplike depression made in past ages by some upheaval of Nature which made a break or sink in the high hills along the Madison, from which a steep wooded ravine leads up and out. In early days The Pot had been a favorite rendezvous and holding place where horses stolen in Nebraska and Wyoming were held while their brands were changed on their way to be sold in Canada. The horsethieves had run a pole fence across the only outlet, part of which still remained, and Old Man Ennis could have told you of an early morning years before when he and his companions had crept down the ravine to the thieves' camp and either captured or killed what was then the most desperate and most successful gang of rustlers in the West.

That evening couriers rode up and down the valley notifying the ranchers, and at daylight the next morning twenty of the best cowhands on their top horses left the Ennis store and headed for the mouth of The Pot far back in the hills. They reached their destination early in the afternoon and found their guide's companion camped in the gully which reached from The Pot up into the hill country, and there Old Man Ennis had camp made and gave his orders. The Old Man's plan was simple; if the Phantom Bull was in The Pot, his only way of escape was through the ravine. If that was securely fenced, he was trapped. The old fence was at the top of the valley at its narrowest point; below the fence for two hundred yards the valley was heavily timbered to where it opened out into The Pot proper. Above the fence the timber extended only a few yards, and then came open country which sloped steeply to the timbered sides of Jack Creek.

During the afternoon all hands set to work to fell trees and rebuild the fence higher and stronger than it had been in the days of the rustlers. Before daylight next morning the hunters had breakfast, and as soon as it was light they were mounted and ready to start beating through The Pot until the quarry was roused. Strict orders were given to rope the bull, not shoot him. The cowboys, with their ropes down, ready at any moment for the chase, set out in a fan-shaped line, Old Man Ennis on the extreme left, Walter on the right, and in the middle Patch Hinton, a long-time friend of Old Man Ennis, who had ridden the Pinto

Horse up from Big Coulee at the Old Man's urgent message.

The Phantom Bull had been grazing the afternoon before at the far side of The Pot, and had been roused by the sounds of building the fence. Curious and half-angry that his pet refuge had now been invaded, he had come up quietly after dark until he was near enough to see the campfire and smell the men and horses which he so much despised. But his escape out of The Pot being cut off by the camp, he slipped back into a thicket of jackpine that came up to within a hundred yards; the dense growth was high enough and thick enough to hide him completely. Here he waited through the night, his temper quickening as his resentment at the invasion grew, so that by the time the line of cowboys started toward his hiding-place, he was as ready for battle as a crouching cougar, although he remained so still that not a twig stirred. He had escaped notice before by keeping quiet in thick timber when horsemen were near, and perhaps he would have escaped again if he had not been directly in the path of young Ed Starling, who rode straight into the pines where the bull was hiding, anxious not to overlook a single chance to win the twenty-five dollars offered by Old Man Ennis to the first man that put his rope on the bull.

Starling's pony snorted when he came to the thick cover, but his rider spurred him in. For fifty feet the rider's head and shoulders showed above the waving tops of the small pines, then the muffled bellow of a charging bull was topped by the scream of a wounded horse, as pony and rider rose for a moment above the treetops, and the great slate-colored bull, tossing them aside, broke cover and made for the trail leading up out of The Pot.

As the bull appeared, the Pinto Horse twenty yards to the right whirled to follow and to cut him off; but strain as he would, the big bull hit the timber before Patch got near enough to throw his rope. Although the Pinto's speed failed to head off the bull, it forced him into the timber a few yards to the right of the

trail, into which the horse turned and the chase roared up the narrow valley on a parallel course, the Pinto in the trail, the bull crashing through the trees fifty feet to his right.

An opening had been left in the original fence line where the trail crossed it, and Patch tried to remember whether the heavy slip rails had been put up before the hunt started. He wondered whether the bull would make for the accustomed opening when the new fence barred his path or whether he would run the fence line in the other direction, seeking a way out. As they swung around a turn in the trail, the horse was four lengths ahead of the bull, and Patch saw with relief that the five-foot slip rails were in place. When the bull came to the new fence, he hesitated for a moment, turned toward the gate, but, seeing the 'paint' horse there ahead of him, turned back again and, making a rearing lunge at the fence, half-cleared it. For a second he hung there, then a post cracked and the fence sank beneath him.

The trap had failed, and Patch knew that his only remaining chance was to rope the bull as he crossed the open between the head of the gully and the Jack Creek timber. He flung himself from his horse, and the cowboys said afterward that the bark of the white birch slip rails was scorched off by the language he used. The delay was short, but short as it was, it allowed the bull to emerge onto the open hillside, with his original lead over the horse lengthened by half.

The Pinto Horse shot out of the top of the gully at a pace that no cow-horse in Montana could have lived with and few race-horses have matched, and was off down the rocky sage-grown hillside as if he was galloping on turf. They crossed a boulder-strewn, gravelly wash, where even the range bull slowed up for a split second, but the 'paint' horse took it with a rushing scramble, and that second's delay gave Patch his chance. They were not far now from the timber, and, as the horse gained on the bull, Patch swung his rope. There was too much sage to risk a throw for a forefoot, and the long loop sailed out over the flying quarry. It seemed to hesitate for a moment, and then dropped over his head. As the noose fell true, Patch snatched a dally on his saddle-horn and the 'paint' horse, true to his training, began to slow up. For a second or two as the strain on the rope increased, the great bull was dragged to a lunging gallop. Then there was a sound of tearing leather as a latigo broke, and Patch shot fifteen feet in the air, and his saddle, like some strange animal, went bounding down the hillside in the wake of the bull until it reached the timber; and there Patch later found what was left of it wedged between two trees.

CHAPTER IV

THERE is no telling what might have happened if Patch's latigo had not broken. The other cowboys were not far behind and probably the slate-colored bull would have gone down fighting before such long odds.

His narrow escape determined the bull to leave his old range forever, although instinct pressed him hard to remain in the country where he was born and raised. He hid in the Jack Creek timber for two days and nights, and on the third night made his way over the Divide, crossed the Gallatin River near the mouth of Spanish Creek, and continued straight through the hilly country until he came out on the hills that border the Yellowstone. He traveled mostly by night and took his time. Feed and water were plentiful, and he continued eastward until about the first of October he came to where the Big Horn flows into the Yellowstone. He made his leisurely way up the Big Horn, and then, where the river enters the canyon, he branched off southward to the rolling grassy foothills of the Big Horn Mountains.

In those days there were no fences in that country. The range was claimed and held by the O4 (O-Four-Bar), which ranged its cattle through a lease from the Indian Department, and probably nowhere in the West was there a finer beef range. Winter soon set in, but there was plenty of grass. The wind kept the ridges clear, and ample protection and good browsing could be found in the thickets which draped the streams when an occasional blizzard swept down from the north.

For the first part of the winter the slate-colored bull kept to the higher country. He could look down and see the smoke from the Indian tepees along the Lodge Grass, and the bands of Indian ponies which stayed along the lower streams in the winter. He was unmolested, for the Indians did not travel much in cold weather and he had small trouble in keeping out of sight of the occasional cowboy who rode the winter range. Once out of curiosity he slipped down in the evening to have a look at an Indian camp, and some squaws who saw the great white face in the dusk hurried shrieking into the nearest tepee and swore through their chattering teeth they had seen a Phantom Bull with a great white face and no body; and the buck who came out to investigate was chased up a cottonwood to return half-frozen after several hours and to confirm the story of the squaws. The story spread until no Indians along the Lodge Grass would venture from their tepees after dark.

There had been no snow, and the frozen ground left no trail the first time the Phantom Bull visited the Indians. The next time he came there was snow on the ground, and the older bucks, after spending a night of terror as they heard him along the creek bottom, pointed to his tracks in the morning, saying that the phantom story was a lie, and, following up the tracks to prove it, came on a worn-out Hereford range bull near where the slate-colored nomad had passed, which they promptly killed and took the meat to camp.

That night the Lodge Grass Indians gathered for a feast to celebrate the laying of the imaginary ghost. Old Whipping Eagle, the Medicine-Man, was in the middle of a long speech extolling his prowess over all evil spirits, when the scream of a near-by horse froze them all into a terrified silence, until Two Leggins, bolder than the rest, seized his rifle and slipped outside, only to come bolting back a moment later, his rifle gone and his eyes starting with horror. He had seen, he said, the Phantom Bull standing by the gored body of his best pinto pony. He had shot quickly — but he never finished; there was a deep bellow and the tepee came down on the huddled Indians. No two stories ever agreed later as to exactly what had happened. *All* agreed that the Phantom Bull had attacked them. Some said it had two heads and a body like a snake; some stuck to the story that it had one head and no body at all; but whatever it was, Two Leggins was laid up for many weeks with a long gash in his thigh, and it was a month before some of the others had recovered from their bruises.

That was the last visit that the slate-colored bull paid to the Indians, and the half-dozen families which lived on the Lodge Grass promptly moved over to the Little Big Horn where there was more company. Whipping Eagle, against whom Two Leggins had sworn out a death feud for lying about his influence over the spirits, got an indefinite leave of absence from the Agent to visit a distant reservation.

The Agent said privately when he heard the story that he thought the Indians had been drinking whiskey and had used the tale of a Phantom Bull to cloak a drunken debauch; but to the Indians he professed to believe it was a visitation to the Lodge Grass Indians, who were noted cattle-killers.

CHAPTER V

ON THE whole, the slate-colored bull spent a comfortable and uneventful winter on the O4 Range. He found the companionship of other cattle when he wanted it; he remained undisturbed by man; and the grimness of a Wyoming winter on the plains was softened by the plentiful feed and the protection of the hills. And then, one morning toward the end of February, as he rounded the corner of a small butte, he came suddenly face to face with Old Lobo.

Now Old Lobo had been king of the range from the Madison to the Rosebud for ten years. He feared nothing that moved on it except Man, and he respected no animal except the Pinto Horse, whose range was miles away on the far side of the Yellowstone. The old wolf's coat was nearly white. The great powerful head and long punishing jaws were more powerful than those of the strongest dog, and he weighed when in fair condition one hundred and fifty pounds. He moved about his range with autocratic freedom. He cared no more for traps than for a last year's shin-bone, and scattered dirt and filth on them when he occasionally passed where one had been set. For the hounds which had been brought into the country once or twice to run him down, he had an equal contempt, for he found he could easily lose them, or, if they were too persistent, lure them into ambush and cut them to pieces. The Honorable Wantage tried it with a pair of fine Scotch deerhounds and a big half-bred bitch, brought up on purpose from his ranch on Powder River. The dog's body was found later, literally cut to pieces; one bitch found her way back to camp, and the other was not seen again — but that is another story.

Old Lobo lived largely on cattle. Sometimes, however, he stalked jack-rabbits, and often in the summer he stayed in the mountains and lived on grouse and deer and an occasional young elk. He was accustomed, however, to leave the range bulls alone. He did not fear them, but he did not like bull meat, which was tough compared to the younger cattle that could always be found, or the Indian pony colts. He usually made the round of his range about once a month, but on his previous visits he had not seen the slate-colored bull, and now his lips curled back with a snarl as the great gray bull eyed him calmly not ten yards off.

There was nothing new or terrifying about wolves to the splash-faced bull; he despised them all, and after one good look at Old Lobo he held majestically on his way. Old Lobo crouched a little, and his snarl of annoyance grew to a growl of warning. Five yards more, and as the wolf still crouched in his path the bull rumbled in his throat and shook his head with a threat to charge.

From sheer surprise that any member of the cow family should dare dispute him, the wolf stood his ground a second longer. Then, determined to give the great foolish bull a lesson that should teach him manners, he jumped quickly forward and five feet down the hill, intending to spring back and slash the bull's flank as he passed above. His plan was a good one, but it was based on what Old Lobo knew of bulls. This time he was mistaken, for as he sprang back, instead of slashing the bull's flank, he landed squarely between the great horns and was thrown sprawling twenty yards down the hillside. He was not hurt, and, as the bull charged down the hill, he regained his feet and, avoiding the charge by an eyelash, snapped savagely as the bull went past, leaving a wide gash high above the bull's hock.

Each now had had a narrow escape; if the bull had impaled the wolf on his horns as he intended, or if the wolf had slashed the bull's hamstring as he had tried, the fight would have been over. The bull plunged to a stop and whirled to meet his adversary, and his sharp horns in their scythe-like sweep plowed a furrow in the wolf's shoulder, for the wolf had followed up the charge too closely, hoping for another chance at the hamstring before the bull could stop and turn.

They faced each other in silence; the wolf uphill crouched; the bull, his legs well under him, prepared to receive the attack from whatever angle it might come.

It was not in vain that the bull's Zebu ancestors had fought the big spotted leopards in the lowlands along the Paraguay in Matto Grosso, and, although he was half again as big as his Zebu forebears, he had inherited all their cunning and all their quickness. He realized now that to charge uphill put him at a disadvantage, and he backed slowly down to where a little meadow fringed with chokeberry bushes gave level ground, while the wolf, believing that the retreat meant fear, followed half-crouching step by step, still wary, but determined now to avenge his aching shoulder by putting an end to the struggle. If he could hamstring the great slate-colored creature and get him down, he could kill him at his leisure and more than even the score against the only animal that dared to flout him, except the Pinto Horse.

The bull backed to the level ground and across it until a rasp on the fresh wound warned him that he had reached the thick bushes. The wolf could now only attack from the front or the side. He realized the bull's maneuver too late, but still blinded with the belief that the bull was frightened and that a determined charge would get home to some vital spot, he sprang to the left and then to the right and in, almost more quickly than the eye could follow. He had worked that trick once before with a young bull elk which stood at bay, and had come out without a scratch and with a good dinner, but the elk had been bewildered with fear; the splash-faced bull was not.

As the wolf sprang to the left, the bull moved his head ever so little in that direction, and then, quicker even than the wolf's spring, swung it upward to the right and the great gray wolf landed squarely on one horn. It was over in a minute, and the cowboys coming by in the spring recognized what was left of Old Lobo, and wondered what animal could have ripped and crushed the great gray wolf and have still lived to escape.

CHAPTER VI

As THE spring advanced, a great restlessness grew in the slate-colored bull, a restlessness born of an urge to find some quiet range where he could spend the summer with a few of his own kind undisturbed by the cowboys whom he feared and hated. He knew that he could find the sort of refuge he longed for on the high plateau where the elk lived in summer, but such a refuge meant solitude, because, while he had a polite acquaintance with the elk, acquired from his Zebu mother, his acquaintance never approached intimacy, and what he longed for was a peaceful intimacy with other cattle. In the hope that travel might win him what he sought, he began to move southward along the lower foothills. Cattle he found in plenty and charming valleys where food was good and water plentiful, but always after a few days he would see a horseman on some distant ridge, or come across some sign which told him that horsemen were about, and always when this happened he moved south again. Early one morning when he was about to bed down for the day, he noticed some cattle feeding not far distant. They proved to be a small band of cows escorted by a two-year-old Hereford bull. The splash-faced bull strolled toward them with a series of friendly low bellowings; the cows looked up with interest at the great gray stranger's approach, but the young bull, instead of stepping deferentially aside as the slate-colored bull expected, pawed the ground for a moment and stepped out to meet the stranger with a challenging roar.

For a second the great bull hesitated, surprised by the youngster's boldness, and then a wave of irritation swept over him and he charged. The young bull was swept backwards, and, realizing his danger, ducked quickly to one side and made off down a little valley which led steeply to the level ground below, the great bull following best pace. As pursued and pursuer burst out of the little valley, they ran slap-bang into a large herd of passing cattle, and so keen was the young bull to escape, and so sharp was the old bull's intent to punish, that they were both swallowed in the herd before either realized what had happened.

A dense cloud of dust stirred up by the moving cattle hung about the herd, and the old bull, anxious now only to escape from the cattle, whose close ranks and steady movement made him sure they were being driven and that cowboys were near by, pushed his way through them and was about to break out on the far side when his eye caught the glint of a bit, and, as the dust shifted for a second, he saw a mounted man only a few yards from the edge of the herd. The splash-faced bull was too wise to risk an encounter with a mounted man in the open level country where he now found himself, and he hurried back again to escape from the side where he had entered. But here again he found a cowboy, and so to escape notice he buried himself in the middle of the herd.

The cattle were driven steadily away from the hills

and although, as the morning wore on, the great bull again and again worked his way to the edge of the herd, he found each time a horseman barring his way of escape. By noontime, realizing that each step was taking him farther and farther from the broken country, he had determined to break back toward the hills, no matter what the odds, when suddenly the herd seemed to hesitate, then to compact itself, and then, just as the great bull stopped to turn and fight his way back, the stream of cattle passed on, and, as the dust settled, the interloper found himself staring at the closed gate of a stockyards. He had been so careful to keep himself in the center of the moving cattle that he had passed with them into the enclosure without knowing it.

For a second he stood in amazed fury, then charged the gate head down. But stockyard gates are meant to hold bad bulls, and, although the stout planks crackled and bulged a little, the big bull came to his knees with a crash. He made one circuit of the yard, ripping out of his way the bulls which did not step aside quickly enough, and then, finding the fence too high to jump and too strong to break, he hid himself again among the others, furious and a little frightened at his predicament, but determined to take any risk if the glimmer of a chance to escape appeared.

CHAPTER VII

THE splash-faced bull was captured in the spring of the year that a British cattle company with an American manager had bought large ranches in Brazil, and, imbued with the idea of grading up the native Brazilian cattle, had contracted for five hundred young high-grade Hereford bulls to be sent to Brazil. It was with a part of these bulls that the slate-colored bull now found himself, but, as he was too old and of the wrong color to comply with the contract, he would no doubt have been allowed to escape from the herd on the trail had the men in charge known he was in it, or as it was he would have been dropped out of the shipment at the first convenient market point, and his earthly remains would have vanished as Bologna sausage down the gullet of some beer-drinking gallant in one of those lovely old places we used to call saloons.

However, his advent to the herd had not been noticed, so thick was the dust, and once in the stockyards the contractor, finding he was unbranded, decided to ship him with the rest, especially as one of his bulls had been badly gored and he was therefore one short in his contract number.

The splash-faced bull made no trouble in entering the stock car with the others, for there was no escape from the stockyard, and any change might bring a chance of escape. He rammed his way among the other bulls to explore the car, and at the first jerk of starting, half-mad with rage and fear, he cleared a place for himself at one end of the car, and, terrified as the other bulls were at the movement of the train, they were still more terrified of the splash-faced demon that stood with his back to the end of the car and ripped at anything that came within reach of his long sharp horns.

The first stop for feed and water was at Alliance, and when the sliding door was pushed back, the gray bull, thinking that escape was possible, literally hurled himself through and scrambled down the chute over the bodies of the first two bulls, which were too slow in getting out of his way. To his disgust, he found himself in another stockyard. He tried again to batter down the gate, but with the humiliating lesson of being brought to his knees. The hay and the water stank of Man, whom he hated, and he neither ate nor drank. He stood for the four-hour stop in the middle of the yard, pawing the ground and grumbling his low bellow, ready in a flash to charge at anyone within reach. By this time, the men in charge of the shipment, as well as the other bulls, were only too willing to give the wild bull a wide berth, and, while the men cursed him for a vicious nuisance, the other bulls huddled away from him as far as they could get.

The cattle were to be shipped to Brazil from Galveston. By the time they got to Fort Worth, nearly every bull in the shipment bore marks of the slate-colored giant's bad temper, and so difficult had he become to handle and so dangerous to man and beast that it was decided not to bother with him further. He was sold to a local butcher and so found himself alone in a deserted stock pen when the other cattle were reloaded.

He had eaten only enough at the feeding stations en route to keep from actual starvation. He was gaunt and ragged-looking; his fine-haired, slate-colored coat was dull and dirty; and the great frame was skinned and cut in a hundred places from his fights with the other bulls and from his efforts to batter his way out of the freight cars and the stockyards. Weakened though he was, from lack of feed and rest, his wild, brave spirit remained unbroken. He would fight now with the same arrogant confidence as he would have fought on his home range in the Montana hills. He had gained perhaps in cunning, but he had certainly lost nothing in courage. When the other bulls had left, he backed into a corner of the shed which covered half the stock pens, and there waited alert and undaunted for what might happen next.

He had not long to wait, for his Fate was coming toward him from two directions; from one direction the local butcher hurrying in from the slaughter-house in his buggy, to inspect the bull which he had bought by telephone; from another direction, Juan Flores, the cattle-dealer. Juan Flores, having finished his business in Fort Worth, and having a few idle hours before leaving for his home in Mexico, gravitated naturally to the stockyards and, strolling down an alley between the stock pens five minutes ahead of the butcher, reached the pen where the splash-faced bull waited. The bull's odd-looking white face, half-hidden in the shadows of the shed, caught his eye and he climbed to the top of the high fence the better to see.

Juan Flores was interested in bulls; what he did not know about bulls would be wasteful to learn; he lived on bulls, for bulls and by bulls, for as a young man he had been a matador of some note and now his contract for fighting bulls enabled him to maintain Señora Flores and a goodly number of small flowers in a style which to all of them was fitting and satisfactory.

Having reached the top of the fence, he walked along it to the shed until he could make out the grim gray form in the half-light. That was surely the strangest-looking bull that Juan Flores had ever seen, and he had been looking at bulls all his life. He was thoroughly interested now to get the bull into the yard where he could look him over in full daylight, and, taking off his sombrero, he leaned down from the fence and waved it in the bull's face.

It has been said that Juan Flores knew about bulls, also that he had been a matador in his youth, but he did not know about the splash-faced bull, nor had he retained all the quickness of his earlier years. As his arm began its swing with the heavy sombrero, the bull charged, and the sleeve of Flores's coat was ripped to the elbow, while the sombrero, with its heavy gold braid, flashed twelve feet into the sunlight and lighted at the feet of the local butcher hurrying to inspect his new purchase. The big bull slid to a stop at the far side of the yard and whirled about to face Flores, while the

latter, having righted himself on the fence-top, gave a whistle of surprised delight as his glance caressed the great creature that faced him. This was indeed a bull of bulls; strong as a buffalo; quick as a panther, and brave as only the fighting bulls of the corrida are brave. Juan Flores's mind sprang four months ahead, and in a flash he saw the arena in Mexico at the Fiesta of Covadonga and the splash-faced bull facing El Gallo, the greatest matador that Spain had produced in two generations. El Gallo was coming to the corrida in Mexico for the Fiesta of Covadonga and the management had told Juan Flores to scour the country and to spare no expense in order to provide bulls worthy of the great matador. But the picture was wiped from Flores's mind by the local butcher, who handed him his hat, climbed the fence beside him, and looked askance at the gaunt gray bull which stood watching him. He did not think too well of his purchase as his eyes wandered over the great lean frame with the immense shoulders and light quarters, and it took but little bargaining to sell the strange-looking creature to the Mexican.

That night the bull left Fort Worth in a stock car and several days later was unloaded in the City of Mexico. Here he remained for the next four months in a large yard near the arena, surrounded by a high strong fence; and as the word of his coming spread among the bull-fighting fraternity, he had many visitors and, gradually, as the weeks went by, he became known to thousands. As the time drew near when he was to enter the arena, he was as well known in the City of Mexico as a favorite race-horse sometimes becomes.

A cowboy, coming with a carload of polo ponies from Montana, saw him through the fence and told Flores of the Phantom Bull on the Madison. The story spread and was embroidered and enlarged upon and finally attached itself to the splash-faced bull, until he began to assume an almost legendary character in the minds of the lower classes and he began to be called 'El Fantasmo' — The Phantom. The newspapers, encouraged by the management, got hold of the story, and the week before the Fiesta played up the theme daily, so that by the time the great day arrived El Fantasmo had become, in the minds of the people, almost heroic.

El Gallo came a week before he was to appear in

the arena. He was the spoiled darling of Spain. He made no secret of his contempt for the Mexicans, whom he regarded as barbarians; and he spoke of the Mexican bulls with unmeasured scorn. He strutted and swaggered about the city and gave interviews to the newspapers, boasting of his prowess, until the public and the press, smarting under his contempt and disgusted with his boasts, came to the arena on the great day anxious only to see their country vindicated. As their bitterness against El Gallo grew and the legend of El Fantasmo spread, the Mexicans began to feel that the great gray bull was Mexico's champion against the supercilious Spaniard. Never in the history of bull-fighting in Mexico had feeling and excitement run so high. The vast arena was jammed to the danger point, and so high was the feeling against El Gallo that he was escorted to the arena by a squadron of police, for fear he might be mobbed by the crowds who, unable to obtain seats, waited outside, irritated to the point of violence by El Gallo's assumption of Spanish superiority.

CHAPTER VIII

WHEN El Gallo entered the ring for the first bull, there was not a sound of applause from the spectators, and El Gallo, with a sneer, doffed his hat to the President's box. The first bull was a small reddish animal, neither aggressive, vicious, nor fast, and after a few moments' play the Spaniard, finding that he could get no response, walked to within five inches of the bull's nose, and then, deliberately and with a gesture of disdain, turned his back on his antagonist and walked out of the arena. The Mexicans groaned. The second bull was little better, and again El Gallo stalked out of the arena, refusing to soil his sword in the carcass of so worthless a victim.

The third bull, nearly black, but shading off to a rich tan on his belly and legs, was of a better breed. A flicker of excitement passed through the crowded benches as the black bull threw and gored a horse, and a ripple of unwilling applause broke out as, accepting the challenge of El Gallo, he charged. The great bull-fighter, pirouetting on his toes, like a dancer, allowed the bull's sharp horns to slip past within two inches of his body. At the end, El Gallo killed him with a clean thrust between the shoulders. It was neatly done, but the crowd's applause was more for the Mexican bull that had fought and lost than for the Spaniard who had fought and won.

The fourth bull, another red one, was like the first

and second, and El Gallo left the ring in disgust, allowing a local bull-fighter to give the final thrust. The spirits of the crowd sank again. 'Were there no bulls in the New World which could make this supercilious Spanish shrimp show his wares?'

The fifth bull was better, and in the first few minutes the crowd sat up and took notice, for this bull, like the black bull, accepted every challenge and El Gallo came to life. Once, when the bull stood facing him, head down, ready to charge, he diverted the bull's eye for a second with his cape and in the same instant stepped coolly onto the bull's lowered head and, before the bull knew what had happened, skipped lightly as a blown thistle onto and off the bull's back. But the excitement died down after that; the bull seemed cowed and bewildered and stood sullen, and with difficulty was maneuvered into a favorable position so that El Gallo could kill him with that deliberate, accurate thrust. Then, when he had been dragged out by the gayly bedecked mules with their tinkling bells and the ground of the arena had been freshly sanded and smoothed, the gate of the bullpen swung open and the crowd sprang to its feet, shouting 'Viva Mexico!' — 'El Fantasmo!' — 'El Fantasmo!' as the Phantom Bull trotted into the arena.

El Fantasmo stared about him in surprise. What did it all mean? — the mounted picadores on their blindfolded horses and the bright tier on tier of spectators which rose about him on all sides? He stared with suspicion at the word 'Covadonga' written out in red and yellow sawdust in letters ten feet long on the smooth sand of the arena. He lowered his head to sniff at them and a maddening smell of blood came to his nostrils. Then, as a gayly dressed capeador, flaunting a crimson cape, left the barrier and came toward him, he charged. The capeador, taken by surprise at the sudden fury of the attack, turned and ran to gain the protection of the barricade, but he was a second too slow and he was hurled ten feet in the air and landed on the laps of the spectators on the lower tier of seats. The bull, hardly checking his speed, turned and charged the nearest horseman; horse and man went down in a heap, and the bull, with his long sharp horns buried in the horse's belly, ripped and tore the unfortunate creature to pieces. The next nearest picador spurred up to divert the bull's attention, and, as the bull felt the sharp prick of his long lance, he turned from the prostrate horse and charged his enemy. So sudden and vicious was the onslaught that almost before the crowd could realize what was happening, the second horse had suffered like the first. The two remaining picadores rode up; the spectators saw for a moment a tangled, whirling mass of bull, horses, and men; then another horse was down and there emerged from the cloud of dust the last picador, spurring his horse in a frantic effort to escape. In the middle of the arena, El Fantasmo caught him and so great was the impetus of his charge that horse and rider were carried twenty feet on the bull's sharp horns before they were flung aside. The final vicious toss threw the man clear of the horse, and, seasoned as the spectators were to the bloody sights of the arena, there was a gasp of horror as the bull turned to the fallen man, who, in screaming agony, was tossed and gored until all that was left was a bright-colored bloody bundle, streaked with dust. The spectators sat in breathless amazement; never had such a bull-fight been seen, even in that city where bull-fights had been going on for generations; four horses killed and a man gored to death in the time it takes to roll a cigarette.

El Gallo was standing at the side of the arena talking up to a lady who, he said, was his niece. He may have heard, but if he heard, he paid no attention to, the stories that for a week had been circulating through the city about the Phantom Bull. He despised all Mexicans; he despised their bulls; he regretted that he had allowed the lure of gold to take him, if only for a while, to a country of barbarians which neither knew nor appreciated a bull-fighter when they had the chance. He was aggrieved as he recalled the applause, the deference — yes, the adulation even which his presence always evoked in Sevilla and Madrid. He was saying to his niece that he had been a ten-headed fool to come; that she had been a ten times ten-headed fool to advise him to come; that she need not put on airs because the rich young Mexican in the opposite box had smiled at her; they would go home tomorrow, and he would show her, when they got to Spain, that El Gallo was not to be treated like a common mule-driver of the corrida. He was going to say a lot more

when the tail of his eye caught the Phantom Bull as he came to a stop in the middle of the arena.

The niece looked down and pointed with her fan. 'There, my friend,' she said, 'is a *bull;* go and meet him.'

El Gallo nodded and threw his cigarette away. 'He should be a work ox in Andalusia,' he said, 'but anything is better than watching you make a fool of yourself with these paysano dandies.' He added, with ironical courtesy, as he turned toward the arena, 'If you care to divert your eyes for a few moments from that young gentleman, I shall show you, along with this gallery of fools, that a real matador can not only kill a bull, but can play him as well'; and he walked to the center of the ring.

El Fantasmo stared about him for a new victim, but his sides were heaving; the past few months of idleness in the hay corral had softened him, and the pace of the battle had begun to tell. Then, as he lowered his head and sniffed the blood-stained ground, El

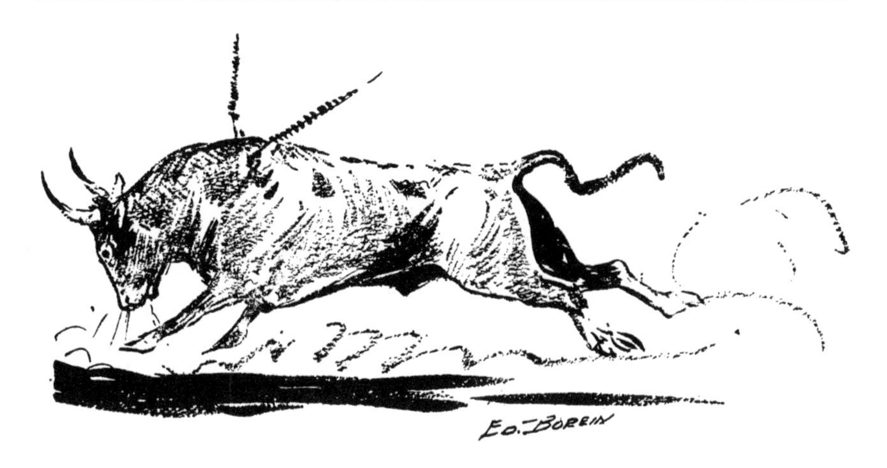

Gallo walked toward him, his light blue jacket and trousers sparkling with silver braid. He snatched from the banderillero the banderillas with gay streamers which fluttered a little as he walked. He stepped to within ten feet of the bull and kissed his hand to the box where his niece was sitting, while El Fantasmo stared in surprise at the only living creature which for years had not seemed to fear him. El Gallo bowed to the bull. 'My friend,' he began — but he never finished, for without a split-second's warning the bull charged. At the same instant, El Gallo turned half-around, his body swaying ever so little, and the bull passed by him with the banderillas now sunk in his great shoulders. The crowd stood up and yelled its applause and appreciation, for the quickness of the charge was unparalleled and El Gallo's execution was perfection. El Gallo, however, did not come out of it quite unscathed; he had not quite allowed for those long upward-sloping horns. His right sleeve was ripped from wrist to shoulder and a deep red furrow, the length of his arm, on the under side marked the bull's score.

The bull plunged to a stop, whirled, and now faced his adversary again, while El Gallo ripped off his torn sleeve, rolled it into a bloody ball, and, with a gesture of disdain, tossed it in the bull's face. His arm ached, but he knew until the wound began to stiffen it was as good as ever. He fluttered his scarlet cape almost to touch El Fantasmo's nose and the bull charged again. Was it a dim memory of the fight with the grizzly that spring morning in the Montana meadow, or was it an instinctive cunning inherited from his Zebu forebears? — for this time, the bull, ignoring the cape, charged the man, and not where the man was, but where he would be. El Gallo was forced to step a pace backwards as the bull passed under his arm. The crowd yelled more wildly, but whether for the man or the bull it was hard to say, for, although El Gallo was still standing, apparently untouched, he had been forced to retreat and it was seen that his jacket had been torn clear across the front above the waistline. Another eighth of an inch and El Gallo would have been gasping his life out. The bull turned to face his adversary, but El Gallo's clothes hung in shreds, unbecoming the dignity of the greatest matador in Spain, and at a sign from him the gate at the end of the arena opened and two picadores spurred in their snorting, unwilling horses, and four or five gayly dressed capeadores sprang from the barricades.

Why give the horrid details of what followed? In two minutes both horses were kicking out their death agony; the capeadores were behind the barricade again, except one unfortunate who, remaining in the ring too long, was now flying for his life to the barrier, with El Fantasmo not twenty feet behind. The man jumped to the top of the four-foot barricade and paused there, breathless, thinking himself safe, but the gray bull, blind now with fury, heaved his great bulk at the obstacle, cleared it with his front legs, hung for a moment suspended, and then crashed into the gangway on the other side, crushing the man, who, knocked from the top of the fence, had fallen underneath him. The bull scrambled to his feet and started trotting around the gangway which circles the arena on the outside, while the crowd, mad with terror lest he climb into the lower seats, trampled each other as those on the lower tiers sought safety higher up. The fall over the barricade, however, had knocked out what little wind remained to the great bull and he sought now only for escape from a place which had become a burning terror. He circled the gangway until he found an opening which apparently gave him access to freedom and through it he went, only to find himself back again in the arena, which he now both hated and feared. He was exhausted now; his great sides heaved like bellows; his breath came in sobbing gasps; streams of thick saliva and foam dripped from his open mouth and lolling tongue, and his eyes, blood-shot and sunken, were glazing with exhaustion. He staggered to the center of the arena and stopped, his legs apart, his great, bloody head nearly touching the ground. Then, El Gallo, redressed, refreshed, his aching arm bound tightly to dull the pain, entered the arena, and this time the crowd knew he had come to kill, for he carried, wrapped in his cape, the sword which they had seen him use with such precision and skill.

El Gallo had realized, in his first encounter with El Fantasmo, that his reputation was at stake, and he knew that until the bull was exhausted by more fighting, it was risking his reputation and perhaps his life to attempt the coup de grace. Now things were as he wished, for his antagonist could scarcely stand, much less charge; he could kill now, skillfully, cleanly, and without risk.

He walked with dignity to the center of the ring where the bull was standing, and with due formality dedicated the bull to the 'niece.' Within five feet of the bull's nose he stopped, turned his back on El Fantasmo, saluted the President in his box, and then faced the bull. The crowd groaned aloud. Was the greatest bull-fight they had ever seen to end without a thrill? Had El Fantasmo, their champion, gone back on them? Was this arrogant game-cock from Spain to slaughter like a work ox the greatest fighting bull that Mexico had ever known? El Gallo's niece sat up a little straighter in her box and, fanning herself languidly, said with condescension to the 'dandy' in the next box with whom she had been flirting, 'Now, Señor, your Mexican friends will have the privilege of seeing a master at work.' 'Yes, Señorita,' replied the young man, 'but in Mexico we like to think it more gallant to kill a fighting bull, not one already half dead.'

Juan Flores stood at the gate that leads to the bull-pens and danced with fury and swore until his black mustache smoked. 'Spanish animal, with the heart of a louse,' he said, 'why did he not kill while the bull could still move?' — and as the crowd sensed the bull's stupefied exhaustion, a like feeling flamed through it.

El Fantasmo stood where he had stopped. His exhausted brain hardly sensed the brilliant figure that wavered before his tired eyes. El Gallo measured his distance and then, as the bull did not stand exactly as he wished, he pricked the bull's nose with his sword. The crowd drew in its breath to hiss, but let it out instead in a long-drawn, gasping 'Ah-a-a-a!' — for, as the bull felt the sword sting, a convulsive movement shot through the great frame; El Gallo and El Fantasmo seemed to flow together in an indissoluble embrace, then El Gallo shot ten feet into the air and El Fantasmo crashed to his knees, the matador's sword sticking halfway to the hilt in the heavy muscles of his shoulder. For the time that it takes to count ten slowly, nothing stirred in the arena and the crowded benches were still. Then, as the substitute matador entered the arena to end the struggle, such a pandemonium of protest arose that the President waved the man back, while El Gallo raised himself on his elbow and El Fantasmo struggled to his feet.

'And El Gallo?' — a month later, with his niece, he sailed back to Spain, a cripple with a dislocated hip, never again to enter the arena.

'And El Fantasmo?' — Go to the City of Mexico and ask any elderly man or woman of the working-class. 'Quien sabe?' they will say, with a shake of the head. 'He came, he fought for Mexico, he vanished.' But if you are fortunate enough to get a letter of introduction to Señor Juan Flores, now rich and influential, the basis of whose fortune, it is said, was laid by supplying a particularly vicious strain of fighting bulls to the corridas in Mexico and Central America, you can ask him about El Fantasmo; and, if you are even more fortunate and are invited to his hacienda in Durango, you will note among the Flores herds a goodly sprinkling of slate-colored cattle with queer white faces. El Fantasmo? he will say with his slow smile; 'we do not see him, we do not seek him, but the evidence of your eyes, Señor, will tell you that he must have been here.'

THE END

Lightning Source UK Ltd.
Milton Keynes UK
UKHW020843090721
386819UK00020B/808

9 780803 287525